W9-AEP-883

98.6

BOOKS BY RONALD SUKENICK

98.6
Out, a novel
The Death of the Novel and Other Stories
Up, a novel
Wallace Stevens: Musing The Obscure

98.6

a novel

by

Ronald Sukenick

FICTION COLLECTIVE   NEW YORK

Grateful acknowledgement is made to the following magazines in which portions of this novel first appeared: *Barataria Review; Big Moon; Center: Fiction; Iowa Review; Partisan Review; Seems; Tri-Quarterly.*

Material on pages 45 through 50 is reprinted by permission of the *Village Voice* and Dore Ashton, Bob Kuttner and Joanna Russ. Copyrighted by the *Village Voice*, Inc. Grateful acknowledgement is made.

This publication is in part made possible with support from the New York State Council on the Arts

First Edition

Typesetting by New Hampshire Composition
Library of Congress Catalog No. 74 — 24913
ISBN: 0 — 914590 — 08 — 1 (hardcover)
ISBN: 0 — 914590 — 09 — X (paperback)

Published by   FICTION COLLECTIVE

Distributed by   George Braziller, Inc.
                   One Park Avenue
                   New York, N.Y. 10016

FRANKENSTEIN

7/14 a shadow solidifies in the mist. The cobbled seawall.
The sloop tacks into the harbormouth wallowing in the swell.
Sailor sends them up the bay on a close beat bow bobbing
through the chop while he hauls in sail. It's just dawn.
They're moving into Frankenstein. Sailor finds their berth
heads up as he drops the main halyard Sailor handles the jib-
sheet they come about. He jumps on to the dock Sailor
throws him the bowline.

Welcome to Frankenstein says Sailor I'll take care of the
boat you go on Sailor hands him an envelope.

What is it he says.

A message from Frankenstein don't open it now.

When do I open it.

When you get the message says Sailor he thinks of slap-
ping Sailor's face not too hard just hard enough to create a
dialogue. He doesn't do it it isn't the way. How does he
know you ask. You intuit. That's how you do it.

5/4 The Ancien Caja. How it emerges from the nonsense of
a dream. How apt it is. How perfect. How well it describes.
Describes what. What he's looking for. But only the outside
of it. It's like the jungle air filled with butterflies. Millions
and millions and millions of yellow butterflies a jungle snowstorm of yellow butterflies. Then in a clearing the yellow
flutter thickens clots on the ground a golden clump of vibrat-
ing butter from which butterflies in flickering flecks the
source of all yellow butterflies. Not that. But like that. It's
like the slow throbbing of the fountain of blood in your hard
prick your cranky mind for once asleep in the cradle of your
body. It's like narrow hewn steps under massive stone blocks
at the end of the darkness a pile of skulls. It's like the secret
code on the leopard's fur and the tortoise shell. Emerging.
From the nonsense. Eyelid like a nostril. Stormnuts. Eat my
rubber bag.

7/14 he thinks about the difference between earth and air. He always wanted to be a pilot he no longer wants to be a pilot he doesn't like airplanes anymore. His lust for flight has suddenly evaporated. The chief thing about The Ancien Caja is that it's heavy scaled with rust and mold buried. Of the earth. Still rocking with the motion of the sailboat he's overcome with an appreciation for gravity you might say he falls in love with it. He loves the way it hugs him firm against the ground like a mother. He loves the way he has to press back erect against it his force against its force in balance. He loves the steady pressure of it on the soles of his feet. He dislikes people who are too tall he wants heavy gourdshaped women squat men who look like squash. People who grow out of the earth and never get too far away from it never forget they're going back into it lesson of the pyramids pressing down. Death is power. Only those who know it can survive and then only for a while no escape. They irrigate their soil with blood maybe even yours there are still villages where you don't stay overnight. An *Art News* obituary marks the death of a painter slaughtered on an ancient holiday in the Yucatan jungle.[1] One notes the proliferation in our cities recently of skyscrapers in the form of pyramids.

---

1. *Art News,* December 1956

10/4 ABC network news feature pyramids are the latest consumer craze sweeping the nation an actress rests her chin on a small pyramid while sleeping to prevent wrinkles fruit is said to ripen more quickly inside pyramidal structures wounds heal faster pyramids are beneficial to the health even lovemaking is intensified by the strange power of the pyramid when constructed on the basis of the strictest micrometric calculations.

4/27 Mexico notes he has developed a formula. Love ÷
power = sadism + masochism. "By the time of the Olmec the
early Maya the way is already marked. Or already lost. Still
there remains a big difference between Chichén or Palenque
and the dead weight of the pyramids at Teotihuacán." The
difference between maybe and absolutely. When the Aztecs
take over you get the full treatment. "The captive victim in
his stone cell and the pampered virgin the beloved sacrifice."
They die so we live. So that we live more intensely. So that
we feel alive. "A civilization so deadened by its own proliferation that only death can renew its commitment to life."[2]
A warrior civilization its commitment to life a commitment
to death. She wants to die. The virgin. She wants to fall
asleep in an explosion of red flowers and be deflowered by
god. She's only fourteen what does she know. A teenager.
The priests work on her through sex suggestive stories about
god's potency. Sex and drugs they keep her slightly doped
aphrodisiacs gradually increasing dosage of teonancatyl (pe-
yote). Encourage sexual visions orgiastic encounters with the
gods don't forget she's an adolescent. All toward the great
day of the sacrifice. Death her first real orgasm. He on the
other hand doesn't want to die he's an outsider he was on a
casual patrol captured in an ambush. He sits in his tiny stone
cell at the base of the pyramid all that weight crushing down
on him. His doom is absolute he knows it. He knows it and he

2. Foster Linkletter, *The Development of Early Pre-Columbian Archi-
tecture* (New York: New York University Press, 1948), p. 27.
(Punctuation mine.)

never stops trying to escape. The guards hate him and they want to kill him. They have orders not to kill him so they satisfy themselves with torture anything goes anything that might break his mind without breaking his body. They want him to understand that his sacrifice is an honor a great exaltation as the girl does. Nothing doing. He spends all his time scheming to get out. He's given up trying to chip through the blocks of stone also surprising and murdering one of the guards changing costumes he's tried all that. Now he wonders if there might be some way out through magic. Or through dream. Or acceptance. Or withdrawal. He decides the best thing would be to play his role through. To resist the torture and keep his mind alive and play his role through in the fullest consciousness. Waiting for the unexpected the abberation the extraordinary event the one chance in a million that will allow him if he's alert enough to slip through. Putting his faith in the unknown. When Cortez captures the palace and kills the priests he's not even surprised. He totters up the steep narrow steps to the courtyard where he's immediately slaughtered by the white men along with every other male in sight he's just another greaser to them. Redskin gook whatever. The girl they gang rape she loves it this is it. Like the others she thinks the white men are the promised gods. Later Cortez gives her to a fat little corporal who colonializes her via her colon. She likes it when he makes her entertain his friends it brings back memories of her sacrifice to the gods.

7/14 he puts a dime in a slot and gets a newspaper. The series of murders that turned out to be part of another mass murder now turns out to be part of a series of mass murders. War continues peace continues to be at hand. He drops the paper on the ground what else is new. He gets into his old red Jag. The first thrill is the sound of power when the motor starts he looks at the empty passenger seat he needs a girl on that leather surge of lust steps on the gas a lot harder than he has to the car squeals out. The freeway is already packed and everybody is going at least seventy he stays over on the right christ it's like getting mixed up in a herd of galloping bison. A big Caddy crosses into his lane about two feet in front of his fender and shoots out an exit stupid sonofabitch though he doesn't step on the brakes doesn't have to bastard had good timing. Next thing a big semi pulls out behind him roars past whips back into lane in front of him this time he needs the brakes what the hell is going on here. What's going on is it's a lot safer on this here freeway to drive like a sonofabitch get with it if you don't want to get wiped out. He accelerates starts weaving through the openings hits the fifth lane over spots a speedup in three maneuvers over through a gap then back to four to three to one to three again moving along the five lanes between seventy-five and eighty like the notes along a sheet of music shit he loves it he tunes the radio on to some heavy rock. He isn't too smart damn him. He goes to sea in a small boat he goes into the desert he goes into the jungle and he finds out about The Ancien Caja. When he comes back he knows as well as I do that the country is racing like a wheel out of contact with the ground a loose flywheel spinning faster and faster till it tears the whole machine apart. He swears he's going to slow down do everything slowly breathe deep stay calm. Now look at him driving like a maniac horny as a toad that's part of the mania. That and the music and all the funny pills. Suddenly he realizes he's eyeball to eyeball with The Problem. He pulls over into the right lane slows down. Either way you pay he thinks he thinks of the loose wheel The Ancien Caja his lost calm. Ancien Caja or Red Jag either way you choose you lose. It's all geschrefftig. Schleissbaden. Shnoch. Now he knows he's back in his life and after all he's learned everything is the same as before. Only worse.

10/23 he has a thing and that is that he's only interested in
the extraordinary. He thinks that the extraordinary is the
answer to The Problem. For example he'd rather sit home
and watch the hummingbird at the feeder outside his window
than go through the motions of a common seduction with
nothing special about it. Hummingbirds are special birds the
way dolphins are special animals they have a certain perspec-
tive a kind of openendedness about their intelligence that
makes him feel kin. Ariel was a hummingbird. He believes
in powers meaning the extension of the ordinary to the point
of the incredible and he believes that these powers are real
though they can't be willed and they belong to everyone who
isn't blinded by the negative hallucination of our culture. A
negative hallucination is when you don't see something that's
really there. He still has negative hallucinations but is trying
to get rid of them. Like when The Witch suddenly says what
he's thinking he never bothers to ask how did you know. Or
when something is lost and he inexplicably knows where it is
he no longer finds it disturbing. Or when he walks into a store
in New York to buy a pair of shoes and he meets a friend he
hasn't seen in five years and who is in Paris and only passing
through the city for two hours neither are surprised because
this kind of thing happens to both of them all the time. He
believes that to get rid of negative hallucination you have to
be enchanted. He believes that all people need to enchant
their lives but that only those succeed who neither search nor
close their minds but simply remain open to the unknown.
He thinks that this is the source of all civilization. People also
have the power to enchant one another and when this hap-

pens they are what he refers to as in touch. When people are not in touch it's dull and sometimes painful. It's even possible for people to be out of touch with themselves and he now believes that when this occurs on a mass scale as he thinks it has the only resort is to The Ancien Caja. But even he doesn't know what The Ancien Caja is. Exactly. There's also the possibility that it isn't exact. All he knows about it for sure is that it's extraordinary. The extraordinary. At one time people in Frankenstein thought that the answer might be sex but people were confused the answer is not sex. He now understands that they were confusing sex with the extraordinary but it's not sex that's extraordinary it's the extraordinary that's extraordinary. The point is that sex is the only thing we can't do without that has to be either extraordinary or hellish so it brings up all the problems. In the long run there's only love and hate. Well if you can't go around it go through it. That's how you do it.

8/19 magic portholes through the clopclop. He sits at a table in a hamburger palace reading the paper. At first he ignores the itching in his back. Then he rubs at it with one finger finally he drops his paper and does a real job. He returns to his paper. The itching comes back. Just as he's about to go up under his shirt a hot-icy prickling spreads across his back that makes his spine quiver and jerk. The itch is gone but then he feels a soft tickling on the back of his neck. He rubs his neck it recedes he goes back to his paper. Abruptly he drops the paper on the table his body turns around on the chair as if he's undergoing some sort of tropism and there at a table behind him is a beautiful woman staring deeply at him her eyes two soft brown daubs of chocolate and not only that she has a halo. He does a doubletake when he looks again the halo is gone. He changes his seat so he can look at her she's staring at her plate finally she meets his glance when the waitress comes with his sandwich he points to her says Put it over there and follows the sandwich to her table.

Okay?

Okay she answers. This isn't like him he never does this sort of thing some kind of electricity is running through him when he sits down with her his whole body is shaking. How did you do that he says.

What.

Make me look at you.

I'm a witch

A good witch or a bad witch.

Both

Then I guess I'm in for it.

But from her point of view it seems like this this unusual looking man walks into the restaurant with eyes that appear to be looking through the walls or into his own brain. And he seems filled with power not kinetic or directed power but potential. Contained power. Something in the way he moves or carries himself maybe. Or his eyes. And she feels the power as he sits there oblivious to her feels drawn toward his forcefield as though by a tangible magnetic current so she concentrates on him by focussing on his back. She believes she can make her friends come to her when she wants them through some kind of telepathy but she's never tried this before. Getting in touch with a stranger by concentrating directly at him far out when he comes over she already belongs to him has gone to bed with him is irrevocably connected with him forever it's just a question of joining in the elaborations of that hypnotic dance whose choreography was determined when they first looked into one another's eyes. During their first sublime sexual consummation which occurs that same day she revels in her submission enchants herself with the feeling that she is taking off her clothes in front of someone out of another order of existence who she will serve and please with all her acute witchy intuition as he tells her what to do. Someone at last from the realm of certitude and infallibility that heaven of perfection she always knew existed. For this later there would be hell to pay.

Love conks us all.

10/25 he and The Witch are seeing a movie. The movie is about themselves it's their life. The theme of the movie is the extraordinary they want their life to be extraordinary something really special luminous vibrant everybody does like when you fall in love. His way of doing this is by falling in love all the time. Simple. You said it. That's before meeting The Witch after he meets The Witch he can't fall in love all the time because he's already in love. That's fine but there's one thing about movies and that is they have to move. For a while they move in and as they move in they have many extraordinary moments like any two lovers moving into one another that doesn't make them any less extraordinary. They move in as far as they can move in that direction until they're almost more like brother and sister than lover and lover then they start moving out. And as they move out they also have many extraordinary moments cut to him and The Witch visiting her friend Elizabeth and her new husband Ned. Are you Elizabeth he says when she greets them at the door. Medium close up of his face as he tries to connect this bigeyed jiggle-tit jellyass physical presence with the disembodied intelligence and its ongoing series of unsettled problems that The Witch talks about as Elizabeth. Ned seems pleasantly drunk. The hello embrace he gives The Witch lasts an instant too long and the intimacy of his handshake and smile as if they share something makes him wonder whether he ever slept with her. They are entering a phase in their affair when power relations are shifting he is no longer god the father not that he ever wanted to be it's just that she resents that he ever was. The Witch is into women's liberation cultivating

her witchy potency. He understands wondering about Ned
that she might no longer always tell him the truth or rather
that she might consider that the truth is not always his business. Whatever it is it's immediately clear to him that some
kind of enchantment is taking place some kind of special current is circulating among them something very strong it's
coming in from Elizabeth sitting on the floor to his left and
it's going out to The Witch on his right sometimes it reverses
direction pan around circle. He knows Elizabeth wants to
make love with him he can see the same thing working between Ned and The Witch and he doesn't exactly like it. But
he sort of likes it. He likes the way everything is multiplied
by four the tension is almost unbearable not quite and besides he has the exhilarating feeling with these two that they
understand everything no waste. Not everything almost everything minimal waste and the joints go round and the records
go round and round and they dance to the music. Except
they aren't dancing. Except they are. As they talk they begin
to leave out the connections between thoughts then they
begin to leave out the thoughts everyone understands
effortlessly it feels like Superman leaping tall buildings
at a single bound pretty soon they are communicating in
monosyllables he looks down finds he's holding Elizabeth's
hand. What he feels is a heaviness accumulating in her the
heaviness of fruit ripening on a branch the heaviness of a
breast a relaxation into heaviness as she leans against him.
Fade out The Witch is moaning softly and he's kissing Elizabeth at the same time he sees The Witch holding Ned's penis
solid improbably large against her bare breast a sweet dreamy
smile on her lips thinking this is why they call it little man
at the same time as quondam tonsils and gleaming subway
tracks inside Elizabeth sucking over snowhills blessing aero-
space and hot baked bean sauce at the same time as The
Witch grunting and hissing like a furious animal at the same
time he bellywops into starguts.[3]

---

3. "In the period '60 - '69 all categories termed 'sexual experiment'
describe a rising curve whose components vary with different segments
of the population. According to Wertz's sample in 1969 these categories accounted for at least 6 to 11 percent of the total orgasms of the
female college educated population between 18 and 40." F. Klein
and B. Wilson, "Sexual Experiment and Social Change." *Behavior*, XIV,
2 (Spring 1971), pp. 453-454. (Punctuation mine.)

No date transcript *sound of door closing.*
Why is the recorder on.
Where've you been all night.

You look like you've been swimming all night.
I do. I haven't.
Sexy. Where've you been.

Sounds of moving about.

You've been making love.

Fuck off.
Muffled voice sounds.

Where's your underwear.
Shut up. Make love to me.

Ooo. Aaah that feels so good.

Sounds of panting. Groans.
Turn that thing off.

You look like you've been swimming all night.
Make love to me.
Yes.

What the

What.
What the hell.
What's wrong.
What've you got in there ice water it feels like you're
full of ice water in there.
So it's not all in my head.
Whattyamean.
I had a very weird experience.
What.
This guy
Well what.
Well this guy. He would come but then his erection
wouldn't
Wouldn't what.
Wouldn't go down. I mean after the third time. It
was a little disturbing.
You didn't like it.
I loved it. And I hated it.
Whattyamean.
I thought it was only in my head.
Whattyamean.
His sperm was cold.

10/24 the story of him and The Witch is a story of motion
and stillness. At the beginning The Witch likes to be still
while he moves a lot. The more furious his motion the stiller
The Witch. She is a pliant slave who he rapes when he feels
like it that's what love is. That's what being a woman is as
opposed to being a girl. The Witch is the victim of a long
ongoing rape and she loves it she loves the feeling of being
overwhelmed she loves the repetitiveness of it and she loves
loving it it allows her to turn off some troublesome part of
herself and that really turns her on. This is the story they tell
themselves without of course saying it. He secretly likes this
story it makes his motion even more vigorous more brutal he
feels very manly. He loves it that she loves it if she didn't love
it he wouldn't like it so much. All men are rapists at heart
just like all women love a fascist right. Right. It's all only a
game anyway and has a way of turning into love afterward
and even during. Though it may be a game you can't win
because what would winning be and that's why he also
secretly doesn't like this story because he doesn't see that it
can ever end on the contrary just gain momentum intensity
like a car going faster and faster. He moves faster and faster
and The Witch is more and more overwhelmed he wonders if
she'll ultimately just disappear one day at the height of an
orgasm as she already is tending to disappear as a personality.
So he keeps pushing it to bring it to a climax because without
a climax there's no satisfaction beyond his gutripping ecstatic
orgasms there's a larger orgasm that gets closer and closer but
never comes. And the faster he moves the longer it takes for
it to turn into love no more during sometimes not even after

in fact he no longer loves her at all any more except sexually she's just this terrific sexual convenience he has around the house. She loves that. So does he. They hardly ever have their clothes on he makes love to her hard and mean the kind of loving that makes her whimper and when she comes sometimes she comes screaming. Once he brings a girl around to seduce in their bed while she cooks dinner for them. Hopeless. Afterward he finds it just turns her on. Him too. Not long after that one day he takes her nipple between his fingers and starts squeezing it. Hard. She smiles. Harder. She closes her eyes. Harder. Lines of pain crinkle around her eyes and mouth he squeezes harder she opens her eyes she can't believe he's hurting her this much neither can he why doesn't she scream scratch my face walk out he thinks. Harder. What she does is she starts crying. Deep shattered crying that's when it turns into love again. He lets go of her breast and presses her against him then he takes her to bed making love in the gentlest way he can manage thinking what will it be next time. That's when they go into a new phase.

11/29 that's when they go into a new phase. In the new
phase he stays still. When he stays still The Witch discovers
that she likes to move. Not only likes to move but starts
having long locomotive orgasms no more spring flowers
shuddering open ongoing explosions that rip through her
body and prompt her to reevaluate her life. Every time. And
every time instead of satisfying her increase her desire so that
while she falls in love with him again and again in gratitude
for that hard immobile maypole that she winds herself up on
begins to want other men becomes in fact a kind of consumer
always shopping. For the first time in her life she has no
trouble finding men she likes she finds them all over all the
time men seem drawn to her she doesn't exactly know why
maybe she has some kind of smell like a bitch in heat she digs
that not a nose smell but a kind of mental smell some powerful psychic vibration. Of course she loves him that's part of
the story they tell themselves now not out loud naturally
she loves him in fact more than ever and she has this power
over men that she's always wanted but never knew she
wanted and he loves her even more for being such a powerful
feminine female woman. So when she comes home she tells
him about it. And they make love. And she gives him details
about size hardness width strength thrust and how she liked
it sometimes better than his and as she talks she comes and
he wants it to go on and on and she comes and comes and
sometimes he doesn't come at all but just falls asleep in her
ready to make love again when they wake up in the middle of
the night. In this phase they like to talk about how the
female monkey in heat can have five hundred and fifty

orgasms one after another some crazed rat psychologist did an experiment. This story is a lot better than their last story the rape story. In this story no one gets hurt everyone has fun. He has a perpetual erection she has a continuous orgasm it's really the woman who needs a lot of men not the other way around. The Witch goes full throttle no longer does she suppress her power big hot spermsucking manmother. So they push it. To climax. Spike's going to come live here for a while.

What's so great about Spike.

Guess.

Spike walks in and she shows him to their bed he sleeps on the couch listening to their love sounds now and then she calls him in. Spike's not a bad guy polite friendly outfront. He doesn't talk very much he likes to eat. His favorite phrase is Well let's get it on. They get it on for almost a week it's really great because she really prefers Spike to him right now but she really loves him and that makes it cool. And he really likes Spike even loves him sort of by extension and one day he decides to explain this to Spike but when he opens his mouth what comes out is When you gonna get the hell outa here. So Spike leaves and The Witch figures that's okay because she really loves him and she digs into her feeling of that love but the feeling doesn't come and she digs deeper and it doesn't come and it doesn't come and it doesn't come. And she doesn't love Spike either and the manmother doesn't love any of her men and he is pissed off and she feels like she's dead and he knows they blew it and he packs his things walks out and tries to think about The Ancien Caja.

4/28 the following situation is revealed to him. A man and
a woman live together with their daughter who has just
reached puberty. The man has worked hard to arrive at his
current state of security. He and his wife are survivors of the
Nazi camps. They live in a fairly comfortable apartment in a
large city in Frankenstein. When they sit around their dinner
table together their tone might best be described as grim
satisfaction. One evening the girl and her mother sit talking
seriously just before the father comes home. The problem
they talk about is the series of oppressive harassments that
have occurred in the household of a poltergeist nature.
Glasses break without being touched appliances fail then the
next minute work perfectly furniture in the next room is
knocked around. The oven cooking the roast is turned off
and at dinnertime they find the meat raw. They wake up to
find the windows cracked the thermostat broken the house
cold. A vase smashes to the floor as they begin Sunday dinner
the bed collapses as they brush their teeth at night nothing is
ever where they left it. Their feelings have evolved from
annoyance to paranoia. They are mystified and helpless yet
the two females feel an impulse to protect the father from
the situation as much as possible realizing instinctively that
he is the most vulnerable to it. As they talk the mother tends
to agree with her husband's theory that these strange phe-
nomena represent the return of their guilt for having escaped
the camps. The daughter on the other hand says this is
nonsense she's had nothing to do with the camps feels no
guilt about them yet these things are happening to her too.
When they hear the father coming in they fall silent and

concentrate on their sewing. One day the father is approached by an Italian from whom he learns that the only way he can escape the situation is by making a deal with the underworld. For the price of some vague agreement to be cooperative he will gain the power to handle the harassments. However he is extremely hesitant to make such an agreement because he knows that once he makes a deal with the underworld he'll never get away from it. Of course he's aware of the general theory about poltergeists as the consequence of the sudden influx of vital energy after puberty which the adolescent can't deal with and so projects in destructive forms. But this says nothing to him because he feels that the camps were the consequence of precisely the same phenomenon of life energy in the absence of creative forms turning against itself. Finally he decides that life is always full of danger anyway. Since he can't deny the existence of the underworld he'd best come to terms with it. He'll make the deal and handle problems with the underworld when they come up. He thinks he can face the underworld cooperate with it even use it and still retain his own identity. In any case life is a continual process of problems that arise and somehow have to be dealt with. He feels his decision is a mature one.

Is he right.

Is there a difference between the Germans and the Italians.

Is his daughter working for the underworld.

12/17 spends the whole day watching for whales. None
come. He feels dry and constipated if you know that feeling
it's what he likes to call the no whale feeling. It's like fishing
all day and not catching a thing not even getting a bite. Angst
held static by angst. He has this thing with whales here on the
extreme western edge of Frankenstein the whales come by
every year. He feels a special relation with them that he can
tell when they're going to appear then he waits at some look-
out with his binoculars it is a kind of fishing a kind of psychic
fishing. The spouts are gigantic ejaculations of course he
knows it's just breathing but it's special breathing the exhala-
tions of the largest living animals at fifteen minute intervals
is not just ordinary breathing it's more like victory rockets
shooting up from floating football fields orgasms in celebration of life by bulk life. He thinks of the eerie ecstacy of
whale songs calm throbbing poignant that's the kind of song
he wants to compose he's starting a new career he wants to
be a songwriter but he's stuck. He wants to write lyrics without words that presents a tough problem for a songwriter
because as he knows we live in words words are the water we
swim in he wants to move to the subverbs is the way he puts
it and he can't even move his vowels. See it's hard. He even
forgets why he wants to do this he thinks it might have something to do with heightening that word seems to have the
right ring to it. Or intensifying. Somehow he feels if he can
do it it will make it all worthwhile make what all worthwhile
he doesn't know. He can't remember. He has these slogans
he repeats like Everyone wants to turn his life into a poem.
Or a movie. Or a novel. But they don't mean anything. Or if

they mean anything what they mean is incredibly stupid. Still
he has this urge he has it simplified at least. A song. One song.
No words. He starts composing pangrams. A pangram is a
sentence that uses every letter in the alphabet once but only
once. No one has ever composed a successful pangram though
they've come close. That's why he likes to compose them.
Because they're never perfect but they can come close. Also
he likes the letters left over because sometimes they form
interesting words words that didn't exist before and that
mean nothing but for which meaning develops because now
they exist. Brillig. Mojo. He believes that one day he's going
to find a word this way that will be the key to The Problem a
word that didn't exist before. Fork jugs vex'd nymph waltz
bicq. Nymphs waltz jig fuck vex rod bq. Hymn waltz fuck
vex prod big sqj. Hymn waltz fuck sex gip v.d. bjorq. Vex'd
nymphs waltz jig fuck borq. Futile. Forget about it. Life has
its own resolutions. Like sex. Like power. Like death. He
calls a girl he likes to sleep with. She's not home. But her
roommate is home he has a brainstorm. He's going to seduce
the roommate then when the other girl gets home he's going
to make love with both of them. Together. This is going to be
really interesting. Besides the roommate is a girl who claims
to be the lover of Richard Brautigan maybe she knows something. Maybe he knows something. I mean here is a girl
saturated with Richard Brautigan's sperm so if he knows
something maybe now she knows it too if only on the level
of spermic consciousness another one of his sloppy ideas is
that lovemaking in one way or another is a form of commun-
ication. So he picks up a bottle of champagne and goes over
there champagne has a certain alchemy about it don't you
think and he is if nothing else there's a phrase I like a kind of
alchemist. So there they are gulping champagne smoking her
hash before you know it both of them are bombed he has no
trouble getting her clothes off. By that time he has a little
trouble getting his own clothes off finally he manages to
unzip his pants but then he notices a funny thing his penis
isn't there. I mean I don't want to exaggerate there is something there a kind of soft little end of hotdoggy thing with a
frill around it it might be okay to piss through but he doesn't
have to piss. He has to fuck. The girl tries to reason with him.
You know I'm usually considered a very sexy chick.
　　I know.

I mean to be perfectly frank men think I'm just a terrific piece of ass.

Yeah.

This isn't plausible. This doesn't happen to me I don't believe it it must be a mistake.

It's a mistake. It's because the whales didn't come and if the whales don't come you can't expect me to come. We're in the wrong movie it's a negative hallucination. We thought it was The Red Jag but it's really The Ancien Caja. You want to turn your life into a poem but there are good poems and bad poems and that's The Problem. Too much clopclop not enough portholes. It's the nowhale feeling so suck ass or jerk anchor. Love conks us all vex'd nymph. Venus. Incalculable. Shoosh Eck.

What's Shoosh Eck.

Borq.

4/29 uptown at the college he meets the critic Mildred
Mittwoch. He agrees to give her a ride back downtown. They
get into his canoe fasten their lap and chest belts. He raises
the sail and they take off down 7th Avenue at speeds of up
to 150 mph sometimes on the thin sheet of water that covers
many of the streets because of the hurricane sometimes on the
roller skates attached to the hull. There are few pedestrians on
the Avenue and little traffic nevertheless thrills of fear surge
through him as the boat catches gusts of wind almost out of
control. Dangerous but exhilarating always teetering on the
edge of control he thinks. She keeps saying that her son
won't be home from school for an hour he already has an
erection and this makes it worse. Or better. He deeply suspects that she wants to make love especially the way she rubs
against the front of his pants. After much trouble maneu-
vering the boat to the curb they park get out walk up the
sidewalk to her building the situation extremely *louche*.
However when they get to her apartment there's a phone call
for him from home. Emergency his father has a painful lump
in his throat he has to go right away. At his parents' house he
embraces his father. He holds on to him hugs him even kisses
him trying to ease the lump but it turns out the best way for
him to help is to take the car on an errand. He drives as fast
as he can to the drugstore speeding all the way but when he
tries to stop the brakes go down to the floor he has a moment
of terror as the car hurtles down the street then by pumping
the brakes using the gears turning off the ignition he finds he
can slow the careening motorcycle in fact he manages to stop
the Harley pretty fast for such a heavy machine. He gets off

tinkers with the mechanism isn't able to fix it luckily a
motorbike like that is just light enough to carry though it's
no bag of feathers either especially when you're not even sure
which direction to take in a city like this. It's discouraging
but still he can think of worse situations than carrying a
broken ten speed bike through the streets of Paris. In fact he
feels it's a good thing that all he has to lug around with him
is his pogo stick even though it's sadly wilted and he feels
terribly deserted being so completely lost in a city whose
name he even forgets.

12/25 the blond comes in two parts. One part comes on a red Triumph 500 in a black motorcycle jacket and tight suede pants long hair rippling out behind blond on leather. When she comes that way he never knows where she comes from some windraked empty Scandinavian tundra maybe sunlight so pale it's almost white like her hair. When he looks in her eyes he sees the greyish blue of that passive sky above lonely men with eyes of slate who wander like brutes gather at random and whose comraderie is violence. Or who she's coming from I slept over at Sonny's.

How come.

I didn't feel like sleeping alone you know I don't make love with Sonny any more.

In the same bed how could you resist.

With Frank sleeping in the same room.

You were screwing Frank last week.

Once just because I was horny one of the things about the blond is that she makes love with everybody once. At least once. That is every man she likes or anyway every man she doesn't dislike and even sometimes some men she dislikes it's a way she has of being aggressive by being passive. It begins when he decides to leave his car on the shoulder of the road and take a hike through the fields. The light is like the sun rises and it's noon and it stays noon till it's five or six o'clock and suddenly it's dusk the kind of day that can happen any time here on the west coast of Frankenstein. No irony no ambiguity No nuances. He walks through a grove of eucalyptus and there she is coming down a path on her blond horse in blue jeans and bikini top he sticks out his thumb.

How far you going she says there's a rifle on her saddle. For rattlesnakes.

All the way.

Alright. Get on he gets his foot in the stirrup swings up into the saddle behind her a nice tight fit with his arms around her waist nothing like this has ever happened to him before by the time they get the mile or so to her father's small ranch the friction is getting to both of them even with the horse at a slow walk. What's she doing living way out here she trains and sells horses she breaks even that's not how she makes a living. She makes a living as a swimming instructor as a ski instructor in winter. Plus sometimes I make a little money racing cars.

What do you do for fun.

I surf.

Are you some kind of ascetic.

Noway.

In her living room they settle down on a big cushion with some grass and a bottle of whisky you drink awful hard he says.

You keep up okay.

Having a good time.

For sure. He gives her a kiss.

We might as well use the bed she says.

1/7 the blond comes in two parts here comes the second part she falls in love with him. It happens during a party of the first part the two of them drinking wine in the sun the wine is the color of her hair her hair is the color of the light this precious light he thinks insipidly but that's okay gloating over the fact that he's not dead. That's what he does when he's in a good mood he gloats over not being dead especially not dead by suffocation under a pile of shit in the camp latrine say or beaten to death by guards after having been forced to copulate with his daughter or watch his wife being gangraped or being thrown out of a helicopter after torture interrogation or having his skin toasted off in a napalm attack or any one of a number of grotesqueries he carries in his memory of the vast culture failures of recent generations. Meanwhile her cheeks are getting fatter something he's noticed before when women get happier their cheeks get fatter he embraces her and as they start to make love an extraordinary thing happens she starts looking younger seventeen fifteen fourteen maybe even back to twelve and suddenly it turns into a party of the second part. But he doesn't like the party of the second part because it makes him skid and when he skids he gets very angry it happens in a second some wheel hits some hidden glaze of ice and he's a very nasty man fighting for control Turn over he says his reflex is to colonialize her as fast as possible when you do it quick like that it hurts them at first but they always end up liking it the blond rolls over trying to figure out what the hell is going on. The blond doesn't understand why he's sore but she sort of likes it. She's never seen him get mean before she likes men when they're nice but she also likes men when they're mean. Not too mean a little mean it gives things an edge she can be mean too in her way her way of being mean is to put her thing on you. Gotcha. You think you're at a party of the second part but you're at a party of the first part and not only that I'm not even there. You think you have me but you don't have anything. Because I'm not anything so fuck you. And next thing you know she's in someone else's bed and you want her back in yours. That's the way the blond gets mean she gets on a kind of passive mean but she doesn't get it on with him. The reason she doesn't get it on with him is because at the moment she should be mean to him she feels a great surge in a bottomless well of jelly that's how the blond knows she's fallen in love with him because that's what love feels like a bottomless well of jelly she loves feeling like a well of jelly Ouch she says. He ignores her he just keeps boring in ouch ouch ouch thinks the blond she bites her lower lip but meanwhile she makes the big jump from twelve to nine to eight to seven to six Ouch.

Does it hurt he says.

I don't care do whatever you want to me she wants to be destroyed. She wants to be torn apart and completely help-less and at the mercy of. That's the way she thinks of it at the mercy of. She wants to go all the way back to animals and past animals to things. She wants to go back to her thing nature and be part of the rest of the world for once in her thingness a thing among things. She wants to die what a relief it's a special kind of death it feels like shitting in reverse no more fighting off all the deadness in the world letting it in letting it in oh god she didn't know she could get this excited like completely giving in he's in he's all the way in he's so far in all the way up into her guts she feels completely owned she wants to eat his shit. He's furious but it's a cold fury. He hates her guts he wants to turn her into an animal into a thing. When she starts moving up and around he wants to stop her he wants her inanimate. He wants to turn himself into a thing a club a gun it's a terrific tight fit sort of opening out at the end he pulls her up thrusts himself further into her belly he wants to destroy her secret her innerness he wants to turn her inside out depersonalize her it's the claims of her personality he can't bear that make him furious. It won't work. Not unless he wants to kill her. She's moving up and around and down he tries to stop her he doesn't want to come he wants to be in control he's going to come he can't stop it he doesn't stop it he hears her cry he comes like a tommy gun. Next thing you know they're embracing one another and smiling. For some reason she chooses that moment to tell him a story about Tommy Angel her biker boyfriend. Once a guy Tommy's riding with gets into an accident. He winds up in a ditch screaming with pain. Tommy can't stand it. So he picks up a rock and kills him. That's the story.

4/30 he sees a strange thing in St. Patrick's Cathedral. A boy comes in with his arms full of large spools he's maybe fourteen blond skinny. The spools turn out to be spools of bright ribbon each one a different color which the boy unreels one by one as he walks around the aisles leaving behind streamers festoons of yellow green red purple all over the church. He assumes the boy is in some way connected with the Cathedral but three swarthy men are grumbling ominously together near the entrance. When the boy goes out they come on with him very tough now he assumes it's they who are connected with the Cathedral. They aren't. That is they're connected with the Cathedral insofar as they're Italian but actually they're connected with the underworld. But they're very touchy about the Cathedral. They start shoving the boy around let him go follow him around the corner. By the time he gets around the corner they're already beginning to beat the boy up twisting his arms taking turns punching him grunting in their swarthy voices Yuh don't put no ribbons in no St. Patrick's Cathedral. He's afraid to do anything the boy is down on the sidewalk they're kicking him he's helpless paralyzed he feels that if he doesn't do something he's either going to have to forget he ever saw this or forget who he is. He starts running finally he finds a cop when they get back there the three enraged thugs are still kicking at the inert boy the cop draws his gun and lines them up against the wall the boy is obviously dead. He goes to a restaurant for dinner and tries to forget about the whole thing. When he's done eating and the bill comes he finds he's short of cash but they'll take a check he writes the check

they ask for i.d. He takes out his wallet starts fishing for his
driver's license can't find it looks for his credit card can't find
that can't find his social security card draft card nothing.
Nothing there. When he finally talks his way out of the
restaurant he decides to take a cab but that too turns out to
be a disturbing experience. The driver insists on going much
faster than seems reasonable to him much too fast. On top
of that it seems that the streets are covered with a thin sheet
of ice every now and then the cab goes into a sickening skid
each time he pulls out of one the cabbie just shakes his head
laughs and goes on as fast as ever. When they get uptown to
Convent Avenue the ice is worse and the cab goes completely
out of control the driver whirling the wheel wildly from one
direction to the other while the cab slides down the street
sideways at fifty miles an hour luckily there aren't many cars
on the road. The driver manages to get the cab stopped at
114th St. after spinning around three times and ending up
backwards. The fare is $7.77. He gets out and the cabbie
doesn't even bother to turn the cab around just starts the
motor and heads back downtown.

1/15 field notes[4] his attitude is why not. She wants to ball
so he balls her. Her attitude is she wants to ball. Baron's
attitude is Pansy's okay she's a real honeybun. Hunk's attitude
if any is not known at this point. Then she starts coming on
with Baron they do some serious boogaloo together why not.
Later he and Pansy are smoking under a blanket in front of
the fire Baron and Hunk are drinking together in a corner he
calls Baron over passes the joint. Come on under he says
Baron brings along a bottle of whisky. Baron has his arm
around Pansy why not before long his head disappears Pansy
starts gasping he's fondling her kissing her Baron under the
blanket Baron's head reappears Might as well come to our
room the floor is a little hard. What about me says Hunk You
don't mind Hunk do you it's his room too says Baron why
not. They get into bed turn out the lights she's holding tight
to him I'm scared she says.

What's wrong.

Strange as it may seem I've never balled two guys at once.

All you have to do is get out of bed he says she holds him
tighter he balls her first. He's lying on his back he feels Baron
climbing on I don't want to do this she says.

Sure she does says Baron.

All you have to do is get out of bed you want to get out of

4. "The subject's evaluation of his or her sexual experience, his or
her intention to have or not to have additional experience and his or
her social and moral judgements . . . have also been recorded and are
analyzed in the present volume." Alfred C. Kinsey, et. al. *Sexual
Behavior in the Human Female* (1953; rpt. New York: Pocket Books, 1965),
p. 65. (Punctuation mine.)

bed. No answer. She doesn't want to get out of bed she wants to get laid says Baron. Then an answer No. But to what question. Then a moan. Another then Yes yes I want to I really want to Baron is plunging he's bouncing on the mattress from the aftershock a series of odd squeaks a grunt a loud cry. The aftershock subsides he feels Baron dismounting. Who's next says Baron.

Who do you want next he says.

Oh I don't know whoever's got it on she says he rolls over slides in comes fast slips out as he rolls off feels Baron's dick brush against him already stiff still stiff swinging back into the saddle he's trembling with aftershock he wills himself to sleep jiggle squeak grunt shake sigh then from the next bed Hunk saying So what am I supposed to do lay here jerking off all night.

Come on says Baron.

No not Hunk she says.

Come on.

Not Hunk.

Why not.

Why are you trembling she says.

Aftershock how are you.

I'm really digging it they move off to the next bed he falls asleep thinking why not why not why not.

5/1 his last job is working on a Hollywood movie. Though he finds the circumstances of studio writing disagreeable and tacky he feels that his reputation will allow him to work with quiet dignity on his version of the script. Nevertheless one day when he hands in his work he finds that all his ideas are vetoed by a powerful studio executive. He threatens to quit. Another executive overrides the veto but it's clear things aren't going to work out and he feels that though the second executive appears to be on his side he's really just looking for a convenient way to get rid of him. After work he goes back to his apartment in a slum tenement. Today he's particularly glad to get home but before making dinner he decides to finish off a job he's doing for the landlord. He hopes that the manual work of plastering the cracked ceiling of the stairway will relieve the accumulated aggravation of his Hollywood job and then there's also satisfaction in knowing that the work he does will be subtracted from his rent. Meantime three Italians are pacing down the sidewalk with their hands in their overcoat pockets looking for the number of his building three louts come to bump him off who pause on the stoop of his tenement and stumble into the hallway almost knocking one another down quite drunk. Now slowly de-liberately they're coming up the stairs their heavy breathing punctuated by occasional swarthy curses as they trip on the steps. He is on top of a ladder in the stairway on one of the upper stories plastering the ceiling and content for the first time that day. The killers pass right under him fumbling panting pushing one another up the stairs. They go up to his apartment on the top floor across from the old Italian lady

who is ironing in the hall where they stand in front of his
door until one of them abruptly pulls a huge pistol out and
shoots the door off its hinges keeps shooting through the
door till the door falls down. No one inside nothing but one
dead cat in the doorway from which the killers quickly de-
duce that he has been gone a long time they don't know
there are two more live cats hiding inside. Somehow one of
the killers has been badly wounded in the shooting. The old
Italian lady is shaking her iron at them berating them as
louts. Patz she calls them or Pots or maybe Putz. Whatever it
is the two healthy louts retreat down the stairway dragging
their wounded lout along with them. Again right under the
crazily shaking ladder with him on top trying unsuccessfully
to restrain his hysterical laughter.

No date it will take him a while after he comes in to
realize what's odd about the party. What it is is there'll be
about ten people there and only one of them will be a girl.
The blond in the redminiskirt and seethrublouse he'll meet
at the door will be the same girl dancing excitedly with two
men in the center of the room. The girl with flushed cheeks
who will ask him if he's a friend of Frank's will be the girl
staring at him from the other side of the room with eyes that
are too deep. And will be the same girl kissing a short dark-
bearded fellow in the corner and then a little later squirming
on the lap of the Prince Valiant looking boy with long blond
hair. Good for them he'll think Prince Valiant Blackbeard
and especially the girl he likes that kind of flow body freedom
easy warmth then he'll realize what's odd about the party.
He will then remember there have been no introductions and
at the same moment he will recognize the urbane vip smile of
an important person an older man the only one there it will
strike him who isn't very goodlooking. You hafv to become
hahrdt the important person will tell him. You hafv to become
ass hahrdt ass what hurdt you. Uddervice itd may hurdt you
again.

Blackbeard. Ever ball a dog.

Girl. Far out.

Blackbeard. Would you like to.

Girl. Depends on the dog I'm choosy about dogs.

The camera follows him as he moves through the room.
The partygoers are sitting on cushions drinking wine and
passing a pipe around. The girl sits more or less in the center
cheeks red eyes glittering and deep her nipples show brown

through her white blouse. A hand covers her breast from behind she closes her eyes opens them doesn't turn around.

A Partygoer. Ever done this before.

Girl. Done what I haven't done anything yet.

Blackbeard lifts her other breast she takes a deep breath doesn't exhale. Prince Valiant pulls her over and gives her a long kiss she's pulled back flat by several hands.

Girl. Is this the beginning of it.

Hands pull at her clothing at a sign from Blackbeard she's pushed to her feet still wearing her underpants. Blackbeard slips a dogchain over her head and pulls her to the middle of the room like celebrants the others form a circle around her. Blackbeard pulls off his belt and gives her a stiff whack across the buttocks.

Girl. Ow. Okay okay.

She slips off her underwear he gives her another whack on her already welting skin.

Girl. Ow. I said okay.

She takes a model's pose in the middle of the circle hands close in pull her down. He has become hard. He becomes hard long before she's passed around to him. The first man penetrates her rear he thinks he's going to faint what he remembers afterward is a rising smell of shit and sulphur. When his turn came he took advantage of it and it was really terrific. He loved it.

He hated it.

He stayed for a second turn.

5/2 Mexico notes Palenque Aztec equals death.

Maya equals death.

Aztec equals the weight of the pyramid on the tiny chamber in its base where you wait.

Maya equals the dream that you can escape that there is an unknown passageway that the pyramid is a dream from which you can awake.

Maya equals the man and woman standing naked in front of their thatched hut at midday in the jungle.

Aztec equals the men with no expression on their faces who close around you in the jungle night.

Aztec equals all in one Coatlicue the beheaded with two heads the twin rattlesnakes of schizophrenia with claws of death with necklace of hearts with belt of skull with skirt of snakes spider hands instead of breasts her talons imprison the earth the war god is her son we are all her children.

Maya equals the parts the many Chac and Yum Kaax also Ix Tab and Ah Puch also Ix Chel and Shoosh Ek and the four Chaques and Ik and the four Iques and the nine inferior heavens and also the sacred tree of life its roots in the world of death and its branches reaching toward the thirteen superior heavens.

Maya equals children selling flowers.

Aztec equals men with eyes like the wrong end of a telescope.

Aztec equals monolith.

Maya equals rise and fall rise and fall rise and fall.

Maya equals escape by water.

Aztec equals flat.

Maya equals fluid Italian the underworld.
Aztec equals German stiff the police.
Aztec equals mastery.
Maya equals mystery.
Aztec equals the stone knife that distinguishes the heart from the body it samples the blood till knowledge is complete that's the way it makes love.
Maya equals the living virgins pushed into the water of the sacred Cenote to make love with the rain god "who don't die though they never see them again."[5]
Aztec equals death.
Maya equals death.

---

5. Bishop Landa quoted in *Guía Oficial de Chichen Itza*, 9th edition, Instituto Nacional de Antropología e Historia (México, D. F., March 1969), p. 11. (Translation and punctuation mine.)

the girl had her red and white dress pushed up around her
chest and two or three would be on her at once sweat and
semen glistened on the highlights of her belly and thighs and
she twitched and moaned not in protest however in a kind of
drunken bout of God knew what until she had been fenestra
ted in various places at least fifty times some of the Angels
went out and got her ex-husband they led him in there they
told him to go to it the girl rises up in a blear and asks him
to kiss her which he does glistening secretions then he
lurches and mounts her and slides it in and the Angels cheer[6]

what would you pay to see a
movie of the Manson Family
in which a dog is killed bloo
d from the dog is drunk and
poured over numerous Fami
ly members fucking what wo
uld you pay to see a movie i
n which a red-haired young h
ippie girl has her head cut of
f by a band of black-capped
black-hooded ghouls on a lo
nely stretch of beach[7]

a pop person is a vacuum tha
t eats up everything he's mad
e up from what he has seen t
elevision has done it you don
't have to read anymore book
s will be out television will st
ay movies will go out televisi
on will stay and that's why p
eople who can give things ba
ck are considered very talent
ed we took a tour of Univers
al Studios in Los Angeles and

6. Tom Wolfe, *The Electric Kool-Aid Acid Test* (1966; rpt. New
York: Bantam, 1969), p. 157. (Punctuation mine; omissions not
indicated.)
7. Lucian K. Truscott IV, *Village Voice*, Oct. 14, 1971. (Punctuation
mine.)

46

inside or outside it was very d
ifficult to tell what was real[8]

reports that several nights be
fore they were murdered Sh
aron Tate and crew whipped
—*and filmed it*—a drug deale
r from the Sunset Strip who
had burned one of them on
a several-thousand dollar co
caine deal[9]

his feet legs head and neck
were covered with second a
nd third degree burns Y wa
s forced to crawl from Cell
55 to the strip cell naked a
nd screaming while those n
efarious canines kicked and
spat on him to force him to
crawl faster when Y was pu
t in the strip cell (that was
filthy as no one had cleane
d it) that has no face or toi
let bowl only a hole in the f
loor no medical care was pr
ovided or given to Y that d
ay he hollered and screame
d in pain the term 'blood c
urdling scream' most appro
priately describes it in that
cell which only has a hole i
n the floor and a concrete s

Manson would get one of the
girls stoned and then instruct
her "I am Christ I am Satan"
he would intone and then "f
uck me you are fucking god
fuck me you are fucking Sata
n" the effect this might have
on a teenage mind completel
y warped on 1000or so micro
grams of acid can only be gue
ssed at[10]

the prisoners were stripped
of all their clothing prodde
d and dragged up the temp
le staircase at the top he w
as quickly seized by four o
f the priests one on each li
mb and flopped over the s
acrificial stone a fifth prie
st slipped a hook around h
is neck and choked off his
screams while the offician
t raised the great knife an
d let it fall a good clean st
roke nearly bisected the v
ictim so that it was then e

---

8. Andy Warhol, quoted in *The Los Angeles Times*, Oct. 15, 1971.
(Punctuation mine.)
9. Truscott.
10. Truscott.

lab Y was forced to remain naked[1 1]

Washington D C for the past 11 years the Pentagon has h ad a contract with a Univers ity of Cincinnati medical tea m to expose indigent patient s to lethal radiation doses an d observe the results the pat ients who were suffering fro m inoperable cancer were le d to believe the radiation wa s an experimental treatment which might reduce their su ffering or prolong their lives the consent form they signe d referred to the dosage as "therapy"[1 3]

if the party was given by so me lord the guests were tre ated to a special dish prepa red from the captives flesh cooked with squash the las t day of the visit was usual ly spent in nibbling sacred green mushrooms and play ing at orgy with nightfall

asy to reach through the w elling blood into the thora cic cavity and tear out the still palpitating heart[1 2]

the walls were deeply sculp ted in the likeness of more idols blood drooled from t heir mouths formed scabby vests there was on the walls such a crust of blood and th e whole floor bathed in it th at even in the slaughter hous es of Castile there is not such a stench wrote Bernal Diaz[1 4]

but it can be told that the y involve relationships bet ween certain Hollywoood personalities linked to the drugs/sacrifice/blood/deat h crowd and certain high-l evel government officials *v ery* high level[1 5]

the Brayton cult is probably best known however for its b

11. Maharibi Muntu (Larry West), *Village Voice,* Oct. 14, 1971. (Punctuation mine; sequence mine.)
12. R.C. Padden, *The Hummingbird and the Hawk: Conquest and Sovereignty in the Valley of Mexico 1503-1541* (1967; rpt. New York: Harper Colophon, 1970), pp. 24-25. (Punctuation mine; sequence mine; omissions not indicated.)
13. Bob Kuttner, Village Voice, Oct. 14, 1971. (Punctuation mine.)
14. Padden, p. 172.
15. Truscott.

the sated guests were secret
ly transported out of the ci
ty[16]

then with an intensive look
of suffering on his spattere
d face he swung upward an
d the ceiling gave way relea
sing a cargo of bloody guts[17]

elief in blood drinking anim
al sacrifice death worship a
nd sado-masochistic sex as a
part of the cult's personal b
rand of perverse sacraments
practices that the Family h
eld in great esteem at the Ta
te house Susan Atkins licked
the blood of Sharon Tate off
her fingers[18]

leave sado-masochism to the
gifted few who choose it vo
luntarily and can make some
thing of it what most of us d
o is just dreary[19]

suddenly a corpse thumped t
o the floor instantly two hea
lthy young nude men emerge
d to hack it to pieces[20]

drugs of all kinds were in w
idespread use girls' breasts
bared to the midday sun w
ere openly fondled[21]

men must act and feel the r
ole of predator whether the
y like it or not women must
act and feel the role of pre
y whether they like it or no
t[22]

Y's body was wet from the
water urine and shit that h

why for instance are there s
till 80 unsolved murders of

16. Padden, pp. 42-43.
17. Dore Ashton, *Village Voice*, Oct. 14, 1971. (Punctuation mine.)
18. Truscott.
19. Joanna Russ, "Letters to the Editor," *Village Voice*, Oct. 14, 1971. (Punctuation mine.)
20. Ashton.
21. Truscott.
22. Russ.

ad been thrown on him an
d all over the cell he occup
ied causing the gas and oth
er chemicals to cling vehem
ently to him and the surrou
nding cell area the guards w
earing gas masks demanded
Y take off his clothes and g
et down on his knees and t
hey would stop gassing hi
m but all the while he was
attempting to remove his
clothes they kept gassing h
im and he was screaming
"I'm going to come out"
he hollered screamed crie
d and finally down on hi
s knees begged them to s
top gassing him I persona
lly don't know whether th
ey voluntarily stopped or t
he fired extinguisher emptie
d though judging by the way
the guards kicked and spit
on Y in an attempt to force
him to crawl faster I surmi
se the extinguisher ran out
of gas Y was also placed on
the Restricted Diet the las
t word I received about him
he is in a mental institutio
n and his mind is a vegeta
ble and he has attempted su
icide twice[25]

young unidentified white fem
ales listed as Jane Does one
through 80 in police files in
California ranging back over
the last few years why hav
e there been at least 44 uns
olved murders across the Uni
ted States in the past few y
ears that have shown signs of
some sort of ritualistic sacrifi
ce[23]

Two county employees today
found the body of a girl abou
t 18 years old on the platform
of a lifeguard station at Manh
attan Beach the victim of an a
pparent rape and murder hom
icide investigators at the scene
said the body had "ink pen w
riting" all over they would no
t elaborate on what type of w
riting it was[24]

"tearing down the mind thro
ugh pain persuasion drugs an

---

23. Truscott.
24. *Los Angeles Herald Examiner,* Oct. 9, 1972, p. 1. (Punctuation mine.)
25. West

50

d repetitive weirdness—just l
ike a magnet erases recordin
g tape—and rebuilding the m
ind according to the desires o
f the cult"[26]

with almost cinematic slow-
motion he heaved his ax alo
ft and brought it down hard
against the white wall inst
antly a wound opened spilli
ng an appalling quantity of
blood on the floor and floo
ding the room with the inex
pungeable odor of the abba
ttoir[27]

a refinement of mass sacrifi
cial technique was apparent
it took but seconds to dispa
tch each victim rivulets of
blood became bright red str
eams washing over darkening
clots like boulders in a stre
am the freshets became rive
rs of blood gradually break
ing off huge clotted chunks
and carrying them downstre
am at the pyramids base f
ar below priests wallowed a
nd skidded about as they r
emoved the bodies that tu
mbled down in ceaseless o
rder the holocaust went on
unabated four days and fou
r nights with tens of thousa
nds perishing on the slabs[28]

I think people are becoming
plastic I love plastic I want t
o be plastic[29]

26. Truscott, quoting Ed Sanders' book on Charles Manson, *The Family.*
(Punctuation mine.)
27. Ashton.
28. Padden, pp. 73-74.
29. Warhol.

5/3 he's working in an aircraft factory assembling DC-3's
the 1937 two motored first modern all aluminum airliner
they still make them. This boy is going to put one together
in thirty minutes says Mussolini strutting down the assembly
line with a group of Nazi VIP's. How am I going to do that he
thinks needless to say very uptight he knows the consequences
if he doesn't do it that is he doesn't know them exactly but
he knows they will be so unimaginably severe that he doesn't
even imagine not doing it. He does it. Aluminum foil is how
he does it and the finished plane is beautiful all gleaming
silver even shinier than the other planes. But inside the parts
are not really connected to one another just held together by
the skin. Just a bag of parts bandaged with Reynolds Wrap.
And now I have to fly it he thinks. He knows the least jolt
or vibration and all the pieces will fly apart in midair an explosion of junk.

Mussolini is enormously pleased. He sticks out his chest
and smiles smugly at the VIP's. Now they are all waiting for
the test flight. He dons his helmet and gets into the pilot's
seat. This is it he thinks as he starts the engines then thinks
again Is this it. Perhaps if before the plane disintegrates if I
pull the silver ripcord that rips the plane apart and if I hang
on to it and if I can jump out holding on to it and if I can
hang there suspended in midair by the silver ripcord till the
plane is done blowing itself apart and all the pieces have
fallen away maybe then I can save myself.

He takes off.

1/23 he feels uneasy. Uneasy and depressed for many hours
now he has been wandering from room to room trying to
shake off this growing dread dread of what. He doesn't know
nothing he can think of yet he senses it as coming from outside himself. There's nothing to be afraid of he keeps thinking
he tries to think about The Ancien Caja lost in the mud of a
submerged civilization instead what keeps flashing through
his mind are scenes from the concentration camps tangles of
dead bodies unbearably sad. The mood condenses out of
nowhere like a fog like an oppressive neighborhood or cheap
furniture or wearing a dead man's clothing. He knows it comes
from himself he wants to fend it off but he doesn't want to
fend it off because if it comes from himself he wants to feel
it. If he can't get rid of it maybe he can go through it it seems
to be located in the middle of his body above his bellybutton
he tries to concentrate on that before long he begins to feel
nauseous. Being nauseous isn't so bad when you feel nauseous
you vomit he doesn't mind vomiting but he's not sure it wants
him to vomit. The whales come when he looks out the window where he can see the ocean in the distance there are at
least three of them a slow fleet sending up intermittent
fountains sounding with flukes upraised bulkheads of flesh
breaking water he takes them as a sign but of what. He turns
around finds anxiety dispelled he blinks and everything is
different that is it's the same but as if he's seeing it from the
other side as if he's passed through a door or a mirror what
seemed the reflection is now the reality or maybe there are
two realities each the reflection of the other and he's aware
of both. Everything is more intense imagine looking at

everything through one eye all your life and suddenly you open the other. Quite beautiful really but this seeing things from the other side makes him feel like a ghost a being from one order of things wandering through another he wonders if he's invisible. As the difference he sees is invisible but changes everything. The dread is there again a tide that ebbed then returned without your noticing he tries to face it feel it fully welcome it he gets more nauseous maybe it wants him to vomit he goes to the bathroom waits over the toilet nothing happens. The dread is the same thing as the nausea located in the middle of his body above his bellybutton maybe it doesn't want him to vomit. Just as he turns away something jerks him up by the neck a convulsion grips his diaphragm he retches into the toilet again again again painfully can't breathe more deeply than he's ever puked before again again increasing intervals again something is holding him by the neck shaking him like a doll something huge but invisible. It has long v-striped fingernails many parallel stripes red white and blue surprisingly Hallmark with horizontal continuations out from the top of the v. Just fingernails nothing else they seem to end in clouds he starts puking again can't stop can't breathe diaphragm convulsions puke convulsion puke painful there's nothing left to puke convulsion puke convulsion scream convulsion scream the puking turns into screaming when he screams he doesn't puke he screams he howls he bellows deep gutstraining bellows bellows of terror they turn into bellows of rage they're the same thing. They stop. It lets him go. The bellows become moans of mere anguish. It goes away. What goes away he doesn't know he hopes it's over. He doesn't want any more he's had enough. Fingernails. He cleans up goes into the livingroom gets down on all fours. It feels good on all fours comforting. Cheerful even he feels like an animal a dog maybe though of course he isn't. He feels like an animal must feel very spinal he likes it. Much more down to earth. Thickbodied. Sexy. Slurp slurp. The chair is breathing he gets up. It's coming back. He has the feeling that he's moving all the way over to the other side. He has the feeling that it wants him to move all the way over to the other side he doesn't want to. Nauseous nausea increases. In the bathroom he starts vomiting again again painful choking again bellowing the fingernails won't leave him alone moans of anguish. V why v what is it is the

question. What does it want is the question he wants it to
leave him alone he can't take any more of this. He feels
like he's moving all the way over to the other side he doesn't
want to move all the way to the other side he doesn't know
what's there but he thinks it might be death. Or insanity.
Something that means you have to leave yourself behind it
won't leave him alone. It's not because of it the moans the
howls it's something else the sickness the terror the rage
something else something very old he can't remember what
was it. He wonders if he's going to die he feels he can hold
out as long as he knows he isn't going to die. Or go insane.
He thinks he might be going insane and that he might never
come out of it that's more than he can bear. That and that
he's going to die if he feels he's going to die he knows he's
going to go insane. He knows that if he thinks that he won't
be able to hold out any more he'll die. He has the feeling it
doesn't want him to hold out any more. Fingernails. Already
he can feel parts of himself going away his middle is going
away his forehead is going away parts of his brain an arm.
Death is flat that's the main thing if his middle goes away he
knows he's going to be flat when things die they go flat he's
always noticed that like a dead animal on the highway he
may pass out. He concentrates on not passing out hard to
breathe he concentrates on breathing there are some people
who are alive who are flat. Criminals are flat. Prostitutes are
flat. Nazis are flat. Hells Angels are flat. It won't leave him
alone he feels he's dispersing parts of him are missing maybe
they're in other rooms in any case they aren't here maybe
he's going to live but he's going to be flat. He's going to
vomit again he vomits again can't breathe pain bellowing
moans of anguish. The question is what does it want from
him whatever it is he'll do it he can't take any more of this.
Please. He can't hold himself together any more what is it.
The terror the rage something that was done to him a long
time ago what what he'll never know. Whatever it is he'll
do it. Death. All right death. It's receding. Whatever it is.
Receding whatever it is it's mere anguish compared to what
he felt before he takes a glass of water.[30]

---

30. A year later he would read the following account by an old Sioux
medicine man: "The great *wakinyan* (thunderbird) . . . is clothed in clouds.
His body has no form . . . . He has no feet, but he has claws, enormous
claws . . . . When I try to describe the thunderbirds I can't really do it.
A face without features, a shape without form, claws without feet, eyes
that are not eyes. From time to time one of our ancient holy men got a
glimpse of these beings in a vision, but only a part of them. No man ever
saw the whole, even in his dreams." John Fire/Lame Deer and John Erdoes
Lame Deer, Seeker of Visions (New York: Simon and Schuster, 1972), p. 239.

1/23 transcript the silver ripcord.
What.
The silver ripcord it's happening.
What's happening.
The fingernails.

What happened. How do you feel.
Every time you laugh you cry.
What do you mean.
And the other way around.
When did this start. What do you want me to do.
Wise old men have big feet.
Do you want me to call a doctor. Do you feel sick.
Peturble me. Horsemadel. Verklimpt.

Are you a dog.
Come on get off. Stop licking me.

The chair is breathing.
Low moans.

Scream.
Louder scream. Retching sounds.
Blood curdling scream bellow moo guttural shouts high
   pitched rising scream falling scream What's wrong WHAT'S
   WRONG.
Better. *Bellow. Scream. Scream.* Better. *Bellow.* All right.
   Bellow. Falling scream. Falling scream. Long broken moan.

Fingernails. Where's the rest of it.
What fingernails.

I think it's going away now. I can't stand any more of this.
More of what.
Long moan.
More of what.
It wants me to move over to the other side. All the way over
    to the other side. I'm frightened.
It's going to be all right. I'm here. Soon it's going to go away.

Am I going to die.
You're not going to die.
Are you sure.
I know you're not going to die. It's going to go away soon.
But maybe I'll be changed. Maybe I'll be flat.
What do you mean flat.
Moan. If it comes back again I can't stand it any more. I'm
    afraid I'll go crazy.
It's going to go away soon you'll be all right.
The question is what does it want I wish it would just tell
    me what it wants *long moan. Long moan. Retching sounds.
    Retching sounds. Retching sounds. Retching sounds. Scream.
    Scream. Long piercing scream. Mooing sound. Bellow.
    Howl. Howl. Howl. Bellow turning into words* What. What
    did they do to me. WHAT DID THEY DO TO ME. WHAT.
    What did they DO. WHAT DOES IT WANT. Just TELL me.
    What does it want. PLEASE. JUST TELL ME WHAT IT IS.
    Just tell me what it is I'll do it. Anything. Please. I can't
    stand any more of this TELL me. *Long moan. Long
    moan.* YOU WANT TO KILL ME. ALL RIGHT. KILL ME.
    KILL ME IF YOU WANT.
What IS it.
Parts of me are going away. What did they do to me. Kill
    me. If that's what you want kill me. *Moan. Soft moan.*

Am I going to die.
You're not going to die. I promise.
Am I going to be flat.
You're not going to be flat either. Or crazy.
Do you think I'm going to come back.

I think you're coming back now. How do you feel.
Okay.

What are you doing with the water.
It's beautiful. All gleaming and silvery. Water is my
    friend. I never knew that before. My only friend.
How are you feeling.
I'm made out of parts and they're separating. It's going to
    come back. If it comes back again I can't stand it. Hard
    to breathe. I can't stand it any more help me. Please.
What's coming back.
I don't know.
I think I know what you mean. I think I feel it what is it.
I don't know I'll do anything please. Hi. When did you
    get here.
A while ago. Don't worry it's not going to hurt you. It's
    going away.
You think so.
I'm sure.
I want some water.

I want to go outside.
Isn't it dark out there.
It's all right.

I have a friend out there.
Who.
Listen. A big strong friend.
Who.
The ocean.

Could you get me my objects.
Which ones.
The rings. The bird ring and the turquoise. The candle.
    The Black Hills stone. The tortoise shell. A glass
    of water. I'm a water sign I never believed in that crap.

Sounds of bedsprings. Is it gone.
It's gone but it can come back the funny thing is now I
    feel it's my friend too. My angel. Only a very rough
    angel.

There is something there though. There's a kind of middle
aged lady there. She's kind of pale and washed out.
She reminds me of old wallpaper you know the way old
wallpaper is sort of spiritually impoverished that's
what she's like. She's nosing around where I was sitting
she's kind of poking at my objects.
She scares me.
Don't worry about her. She's harmless. She's a scavenger.

1/24 he finds himself swimming in coastal waters along
with two or three other survivors. Their life jackets keep them
afloat but he's worried that they'll drift apart. He leads them
this way and that trying to maneuver into the harbormouth
waving and shouting at his companions Over here this way
meantime thoroughly enjoying the salt water the good brack
feel of it. Now and then they lose sight of one another in the
shallow troughs of the long slow swell actually he isn't sure
how many they are three or four impossible to keep count as
they bob erratically into view one by one on the crests then
disappear. When the whales break water like wet cliffs in a
rain he loses track completely. Whales he yells Over here swimming for them. By the time he gets there they're gone but he's
in a shore tide carrying him into the bay his companions out
of sight. The current growing stronger pulls him into the
estuary carries him into a broad river so wide there's no hope
of reaching shore. He gives himself up to its muddy sweep.
The water grows fresher as he's pulled along he thinks it
might be the Mississippi. For three days the river carries him
back through the country to a place where he can see fish
swimming along the bottom and the water is pure enough to
drink. There he pulls himself out on the shore and walks
through the fields to his home. In the house some kind of
social occasion is petering out possibly a funeral has just
occurred. He goes from room to room looking for his woman
but can't find her. He's afraid he won't recognize her it's
been so long. He finds her upstairs in bed with Mark Twain's
great-grandson a younger man an Italian who's taking her
temperature. He doesn't get angry though he feels as a veteran

he has some rights some kind of special consideration. You
might say that he's disgruntled I think that's the best word
for it but in fact it turns out that the young man has come to
present him with some kind of extraordinary award or reward
a gesture of final acceptance. After all this time after the
voyage the liberty ship going down the long trip home. He's
torn between appreciation of the award and dissatisfaction
with the betrayal of the giver. His woman though seems loyal.
Her demeanor implies humility the inevitability of betrayal
and the sadness of all things. Her temperature is ninety-eight
point six. In a pensive mood they walk the young man to the
station. All this takes place in Frankenstein. He wakes up
before dawn knowing the fingernails are present. A face
emerges male stern irascible. It looks like your father. Father
and enemy. Traitor and friend. Disappearing it gives no sign.
When he gets up he opens the message from Frankenstein.
It says Vex'd pig hymn waltz fuck bjorsq. Good luck. Dr. F.

THE CHILDREN OF FRANKENSTEIN

The ocean hunches its shoulder and throws itself against the cliffs. A pause and the wave explodes against the rocks jets of foam shoot into the air high as the over-hanging cliff. Hang there an instant as auroras of spray fall back to the surf. Glittering in the sun. A second later the wave gathers itself over the shining wet sand of the cove skips a beat and slams down on the beach. The waves aren't especially big today the ocean isn't even trying. Its strength is implied in its calm. The surf sounds like a passing locomotive. Its strength is implied in the deliberation of its pausings. It rumbles out like a freight train.

They live within hearing of the surf though they don't always hear it. They don't aways hear it the way you aren't always aware of the blood pumping through your veins. Sometimes they seem to go on and on in the pause between cresting and breaking hung in suspension in a kind of silence in the blank between as when you stop thinking and suddenly hours have passed. Then something breaks in. Maybe its only the way Paul will suddenly think of coming down to the cove to hear it. The way one of them will stop what he's doing just to look at the pines the rocks or whatever. Or something else breaks in. And Paul begins to see and hear what's around him begins to think and talk about it it becomes beautiful. And at the same time painful in a way. Why. The sky an unbelievable

blue as always except for the morning mist the tall pines
jagged to the edge of the ocean cliffs their flat green against
the deep blue of the sky. A Sanderling dodges along the edge
of the surf like a halfback trying to get around the line. Long-
legged Curlews dance back and forth with the ocean disdain-
ful of getting their feet wet. Moss and mussels upholster the
rocks tidepools with anemones crustacea bivalves starfish
soft compositions of pink orange rust different shades of
seaweed. Gee Paul thinks life can be beautiful after all. He
tries to think about the feeling rising in this throat but gets
absorbed in a Cormorant arrowing low over the water and
soon stunned beyond thought drifts up the path to the
settlement.

The sun assumes an odd radiance as soon as it gets well up
in the sky. The weather is never terribly hot but things get
hot. You can sting your hand on a metal pail left in the sun
or sunbathing you burn red before you start sweating. There's
an absence of atmosphere the light slams down on the landscape without modulation simplifying everything loss of
color and dimension. He feels purified and stoned bleached
to essentials as he walks through stunned woods to the clearing. Joan waves from under the canvas flap of the tent she
shares with Dave. There are five tents two to a tent with the
white teepee in the middle. Joan goes back to her knots she
does macrame hangings and weaves clothing that she sells
through crafts stores in the city. He loves her work and
always wears a headband she did for him. This is blond Joan
who he sees holding hands with Al lately. The other Joan is
slimmer and dark and is the one he wonders about. She's a
sculptor and also manages to get work doing illustrations
which she handles through the mail. He and Al with whom
he shares a tent are the only men alone now. If it weren't
for the exercises in the morning and evening he'd be pretty
horny and he's pretty horny anyway. The other three
tents are Ron and Evelyn George and Helen Ralph and

Joan. He wonders for example what it's like where she grew up in Dakota he thinks it's Dakota though he's not sure which one. He knows there was a lot of wheat or is he making that up. The only rule they have is not to talk about the past and that's not a rule it's just everyone seems to feel that way not that they have anything to hide. If they did they wouldn't hide it from one another. Still he wonders about Joan's past and sometimes some of the others and of course his own runs through his head now and then like an old movie the rides the honky-tonky boardwalk. Like an old movie except always slightly different so he knows he's making it up partly. He thinks he's falling in love with Joan. Or something.

The others are working on The Monster. The Monster is the building they'll move into when it's done they call it The Monster because it's gotten so fantastic. That is The Monster is what they call it lately they don't really have a name for it. Or for their group. Ron calls it Bjorsq but won't define it. Or can't. Anyway they don't want anything that defined or crystallized. What's crystallized is static and what's static is dead. Not that they ever said as much but that's the reason nevertheless. You don't have to say everything. The more that can be left unsaid the better that's the way they all feel about it. They never put that into words either of course there are better things to do with words than repeat what everyone already knows. And then you can always shut up of course.

The Monster looks different from anything he's seen before from anything anyone's seen before he supposes. The reason is first the materials available an odd assortment of weathered wood from the old barn they're building on plus a lot of irregular unfinished redwood planks they got cheap so it's a question of following the suggestions in fact the capabilities of the materials and of course a lot of plywood you can saw into any shape you want. Plus everybody getting in on the design like Joan getting obsessed with geodesic domes and George with the tower and Ron with telescoping lateral extensions off one side of the foundation and Joan getting off into multiplying intricacies of a single corner which turns out to be the only corner because Ralph puts his heart into avoiding all angles in the ground plan and Evelyn insists on irregular windows and doors like in Arab buildings she says. And they all agree on a flexibility that disallows fixed interior walls and that allows extension of the basic structure at need or whim. So you get three two story geodesic domes arranged roughly in a triangle with a patio in the middle and rising from the apex a double tower one short one long the latter circled by a spiral staircase with a crow's-nest on top so you can see on the eastern horizon when it's clear snowpeak mountains and to the west sixty or seventy miles out to sea. More like a boat than a house thinks Paul. Or the back half of an old B-17 Flying Fortress. Or the Cyclone at Steeplechase the Funnyplace near his home. But anyway aside from the fact that given the wood and the original barn and the surrounding trees and the redwood growing out of the patio so it looks like the place is an extension of the woods it looks completely disconnected with his past experience which is completely to the good he feels. They all feel. Because there's a sense to their whole thing of new beginning and last chance even though in fact there are no new beginnings and no last chances. Because all of them are leaving behind lives touched by disillusion a recognition of emptiness in plain language a despair at the heart of things so withering that the only answer is to give up and die. That's the best thing that can happen to you. Give up and die. That's the first step. It can only lead to improvement.

Let's call it The Great Depression. Let's say that Frankenstein never recovered from The Great Depression. It was such
a trauma to our parents that it got into their hearts into their
bloodstream into their genes. And now it's in our hearts
thinks Paul. And in our children's hearts beneath their joy-
hunting and rebellion is still that despair. It was the kind of
trauma that can only happen when you wake up from a
dream you think is the real thing and it happened when
Frankenstein woke up from the dream of Frankenstein. And
it's passed in the genes of the parents to the hearts of the
children. Except that Paul doesn't have any children so
there's still a chance for a change of heart. To break the
chain. Bullshit. Everyone Paul knows has a change of heart
two or three times a year some every weekend. And under
every change still The Great Depression. Joy doesn't get
rid of it. Dope doesn't get rid of it. Sex doesn't get rid of it.
Freedom doesn't get rid of it. Murder doesn't get rid of it.
Give up and die. Emptiness is the best you can hope for.
The pause between the beats the clean slate the blank space.

The blank space. Where the terror is. And where dreams
condense like clouds in an empty sky. Paul walks into the
shell of their dream house. From inside it looks like it's made
of eggshells and toothpicks though it's almost done. Or maybe more like a crystallized spiderweb or a glass birdnest. Joan
walks through with a tube of caulking for the panels of the
domes. Paul asks her if she wants to take a break. I had a
funny dream last night she says. I dreamed I was looking for
the real Frankenstein.
Did you find it?
Yes but it was too expensive.
Ron and Evelyn are in the patio also talking about dreams.
This kind of thing happens a lot. This kind of simultaneous
mental rhythm is happening more and more rhythms interest
Paul because he's a musician. Sometimes he thinks of them-

selves as a jazz combo and all that implies. They sit with Ron and Evelyn on the bench around the trunk of the big redwood. Evelyn had a funny dream she dreamed she was giving a sensitivity training session says Ron. What's so funny about that asks Paul.

I was giving it to the commanders of the Gestapo.

I had a kind of opposite dream says Ron. I dreamed Tolstoy was about to publish a new youth novel called *Ketchup on Rye.* The allusion to Salinger was because he wanted to get across to young people his ideas about the importance of being rooted in nature. That was *his* dream.

I dreamed I was trying to have a dream but couldn't says Paul.

Very frustrating says Joan.

I'm very frustrated.

Ron is writing a book. He has a novel idea as a matter of fact it's an idea for a novel. His idea is to write a novel by recording whatever happens to their group so that they're all characters in his novel including himself. And his novel. This tends to make Ron dizzy when he thinks about it so he tends not to think about it. Though he feels he should since their settlement is his idea to begin with and he feels a special responsibility. One of the main things Ron had in mind when he thought up the idea for the settlement besides getting back to earth was to write a novel about it. He feels that novels should be about real life so instead of making up some story he gets a cast of characters and invents a situation for them and he simply writes what happens. What an idea. Only now Ron feels he doesn't need to write the novel. What's happening is the novel. Bjorsq.

Paul's job now that the structure is up is to sand the wood down and put sealant glue in the joints. George is the one who figures out who does what on The Monster. George is a carpenter a tall relaxed blond bearded guy very Coast as they call the western edge of Frankenstein. The idea is when The Monster is done for him to get carpentry work just like Dave the auto mechanic is already getting a few jobs. Paul hasn't done much hand labor before and finds he loves the work. First of all he likes George's reasonable down-to-earth way of explaining the work. Absolute clarity. Paul is with George all the way he would trust him in any situation he can think of. It's that George never forgets what he knows. Maybe it comes from the clear practical nature of work with wood that Paul himself feels when he's working on the building. He climbs up into the sun with the sander and his can of glue. The smell of pinesap oozing in the sun mixes with the deep moist saline smell of the ocean. Deep in time. Or deep into himself. Not the dank rotting smell of the ocean at Coney Island the ocean of his past but something familiar and sweet. The taste of blood when you cut your mouth. The pine tang alone is enough to make life worth living. And the flat smell of eucalyptus of juniper like a good dream when the wind stirs the sunstilled woods or the heavy wine of some flower maybe honeysuckle as he climbs the spiral staircase up the tower drifting into some kind of nasal high. Bark textures maroon scaled madrone saurian redwood mossy live oak. Against the soft blue of the sky he can see five different kinds of pine hard green flat green bright green somber green soft green above the shorter trees. Big Steller's Jays coast from tree to tree laughing and shaking their crests. Quarrels of cacaphonic Woodpeckers. Three different kinds of Hummingbirds whiz around the building a Towhee screes a Flicker drums like something you might do on a bongo if you were real good. And beneath all this the surf like a pulse as he stirs the glue and smears it into the wood. Paul likes working with this glue. It's a special glue made from bull sperm and yucca sap that not only binds but also acts as filler or can make tissue-like connections. Paul works it with his hands dreamy in the sun and a little afraid of falling off his perch on the tower stoned by the heat and the surf sound as he massages the white creamy sticky liquid into the porous wood. From here he can see the snow-peaks floating above the heathaze and the horizon line of the flashing ocean almost lost against the slightly lighter blue of the sky. He works the glue up a seam all the way to the tip of the tower. On top trying to clean his sticky hands he has the impression of helping to create something organic some addition to nature. This thing they are moving into with its domes and towers. This jumbo poppamomma.

Most of the trouble comes from a neighboring group of longhairs. These groups scattered through the countryside have their seasons and this one is definitely into late autumn. For example today at about three in the afternoon one of their men drags into the clearing like a figment of his own imagination wearing white pajamas embroidered with some kind of beautiful intergalactic looking insignia in purple red and orange plus a green conical hat with a long feather in it. He looks like he walked out of someone's dream. He and his friends are from The Planet Krypton and are living on food stamps for the time being. One of the nice things about people from The Planet Krypton is that the women like to ball Earth people like the time Paul gave a ride to a pretty Krypton chick and they ended up balling in the back of the truck. This led to a case of Krypton crabs and feelings of inter-planetary friendship between Earth and Krypton. The Krypton people come over now and then and they're very gentle and lovely people but they're fuckups. Probably because they come from another planet and can't get used to Earth ways. On the other hand they believe in a principle of cosmic energy that seems to Paul very reasonable. They think that cosmic energy represents ultimate reality and that all things are simply temporary manifestations of this energy. The main point of life is to be as nearly in touch as possible with the pulsations of this energy which is blue. They claim that Krypton people have blue halos flaring around their heads and sometimes Paul thinks he can see them. They also have boxes which they claim have the power to concentrate cosmic energy in a beneficial way and they sit in these boxes almost like they were confession boxes or in the case of a large roomsize box they have like church pews. Paul would tend to be skeptical about the powers of these boxes except that he once saw someone cured of a nasty burn in one of them. Unless he imagined the whole thing. Or it was a dream.

In his previous life Paul was involved in politics. He used to be a civil rights lawyer but gave it up as futile at least during what he calls The Dynasty of the Million Lies. That's why Altair always comes to him with Krypton's problems. They're usually of a quasi-legal kind having to do with Earthmen like the grocer and the county clerk and the sheriff. There's nothing that Paul wants to do less than anything connected with his work in his previous life. In his new life he's a handyman or rather he's learning how to be a handyman. There seems to Paul nothing better in life that you could do than to be able to work with your hands repairing things patching things together making useful things out of whatever happens to be at hand old wood discarded bottles tin cans rusty machine parts the detritus of the culture. If he can help it with Altair he tries to get away with explaining to him some basic principles and letting Altair go on from there. Like that Earthmen deal in a unit of exchange called money and a set of rules called law and above all an intangible difficult to explain to Altair called power that has nothing to do with the power of cosmic energy and in fact tends to work against it. Do you realize says Altair after Paul gets done explaining why they won't give him his food stamps that if the Sun were hollow over a million Earths would fit inside?

No.

Do you know that our galaxy has millions probably billions of stars like the sun and a lot bigger?

Yes.

Can you grasp the fact that beyond our galaxy millions
and millions of other galaxies can be seen by telescope? Can
you grasp that?

No.

And you talk to me about money and shit like that I mean
all I want is our food stamps.

Altair knows damn well that he's being perverse. On the
other hand Paul knows that as soon as Altair walks into the
food stamp office he's going to freak everybody out. And
that he thinks if he makes the first concession and changes
his clothes he's heading down a one way street that leads to
wearing a tie and living in the suburbs because that really
gets results. Either that or a power trip like he's a freak but
he can really deal with them cats. Because he's one of them
cats. Which is completely beside the point. The point is that
Altair used to be an addict he needs to stay high. He's not
coming down even for food stamps. What Altair is saying is
that he needs an intermediary an agent or whatever. A lawyer.
Okay so Paul gets the van and they drive into town. In the
food stamp office Mr. Stamp explains that under the new
regulations only families can get the stamps. Mr. Stamp is a
redneck that is a citizen of Earth. For an Earthman he's
tolerant explaining that Altair's bunch didn't register as a
family they registered as a planet and planets aren't eligible
but if they want to register as a family that's all right. But
Altair who can be perfectly practical gets paranoid and resentful confronting Earth's red tape and the general bad
vibes coming from the Earthmen in the office and says they
can't register as a family. Why not?

Because my old lady Cassiopeia took Lyra Libra and
Lepus and moved into Mizar's yurt where she's balling
Betelgeuse and Canopus. So as far as I'm concerned we're
not really a family any more. Paul gets Altair out of there

someone else from Krypton can come another time. It's
not so much Mr. Stamp as two guys with mangy beards and
eyes like pickled onions. Staring at them on the edge of
saying something quiet irreversible and disastrous. Just
before he takes the turn into the settlement he gets a glimpse
of them on motorcycles in the rearview mirror. That night
Paul hears the guttering of motorcycles the distant slow
rumble of columns of motorcycles somewhere in the hills.

The cows. Paul loves to watch the cows over in the meadow
next to the settlement. What always strikes him is the way
their rears end in rectangles. Rectangled and a little raised
like the sterns of old galleons. Their teats bulge like rubber
gloves their noses are pink and each has its own geography of
black and white. The cows watch him with their dumb eyes
and he likes them because they're dumb. He likes the cows
because they're big. He likes the cows because they eat their
grass and they're content. He likes the cows because they
flick flies away with their tails. He likes the cows because
their voices are full and mellow. He likes the cows because of
their heavy slow step. He likes the cows because they run in
slow motion. He likes the cows because they sniff the wind.
He likes the cows because their drool is beautiful in the sun. He
likes the cows because they're at peace. The cows. The cows.
The cows.

Mr. Stamp is in charge of the food stamp office. Mr. Stamp
is also the sanitation inspector. Mr. Stamp is now reminded

of their settlement and connects it in some vague way with
The Planet Krypton which he doesn't like. Things begin to
happen fast. The first thing that happens is that there's a
sanitation inspection. The second thing that happens is they
can't use the country dump for rubbish any more. The third
thing that happens is that they decide to take care of their
own rubbish. Compost heap kindling nothing wasted. This
explains the fantastic decoration of their building for those
of you who may have seen it and are curious. What can't
be used in any other way they decide to use as building
material. Dave makes columns of cans and arches of bottles.
Ron makes huge multicolored designs with bottle caps
banged into the wood. Helen crushes glass and uses the
pieces for panels of mosaic. George makes furniture from
fruit baskets and Coke crates. Al polishes pieces of rusty
metal and welds them into fixtures. Joan fuses colored
bottles into windowpanes. Ralph makes a fence of spare
parts. Joan and Evelyn lay floors of bricks and tiles and
broken dishes and hunks of glass. Paul makes partitions of
leftover plastic. The house begins to look like a collage
made from the wreckage of a supermarket. Pretty soon
they're running out of rubbish. They have to go around
bumming neighbors' garbage. The night before garbage is
collected in town they sneak around emptying citizens'
trash cans into huge plastic bags that they shlep back to the
settlement to sift and sort. A scare runs through town about
"the garbage robbers" and there's talk of vigilantes so they
have to cut it out but by now the building's just about done
so they can afford to limit themselves to their own garbage.
So there it is Coney Island decorated with chunks of Grau-
man's Chinese Theater and Shopwell swooping up to its
double tower like a gaudy chapel to the concept of Bjorsq.

To celebrate the near completion of their house Ron
makes up a song. The song he makes up on this occasion is

part of his plot to destroy the English language. The song
goes like this.

> *Bjorsqi poppamomma*
> *Wocky wocky*
> *Plastic jam*
> *Iron blintzes*
> *Fill the inches*
> *Sooky buby nishtgedeit*

Paul and George are mending nets nets they use to catch
blues and whiskered runion at the rivermouth. Hey don't
you think it's about time for a potlatch says George hairs
in his blond beard light up in the sun muscles undulating
under sunbaked skin as he works at the net.

A potlatch says Paul you took the words out of my
mouth they drop the net and rush over to Ron and Evelyn's
tent Evelyn takes them in with her wide as night eyes. Maybe it's time for a potlatch she says before they have a chance
to speak. They hurry across the clearing already making
plans Ralph is mulching the garden seeing them knifes his
spade into the ground. What's up a potlatch he says at that
moment Joan clambers up the tower and waving from the
top like a spruce branch calls out Potlatch potlatch her
blond hair streaming Joan and Helen down below drop the
apricots they're sorting Al comes in from the woods Ron
runs dripping out of the river Dave wipes the grease off his
hands they gather yelling and laughing at the firepit in the
middle of the clearing mill around the white teepee and do
an impromptu hoop dance. Then they calm down and start
organizing Evelyn goes over to the farmer's wife to buy a
gallon of her peach icecream Steve digs up the stash Joan and
Joan start a stew with the dried venison they've been saving
Ron sets the jugs of home-brewed asparagus wine to cool
in the river and the rest of them work on the meal and pre-
pare the teepee. Soon the stew bubbles over the firepit

steaming with potatoes onions carrots celery chickpeas lentils and lots of garlic. They spread their best madras their oriental prayer rugs their homemade woven stuff around the teepee start a low fire in the center for warmth put the plates on the eating platform start the incense and by the time the light is mellowing toward dusk they gather inside with everything ready. The hash pipe goes around with loud inhalations with long sighs and groans they don't use dope much they don't have time but when they do they dig it. Then the coarse home-brewed wine cool from the river and the stew and the baked squam and Helen's dark heavy wheat berry bread and more wine and tomatoes and cress from the garden and homemade peach icecream. Outside the light fades the fog creeps up the birds get into their last riff before dark deer wander into the edges of the settlement in the chilling air a skunk sniffs at the mulch pile their raccoon comes to the teepee entrance for his evening handout the sun slips behind the ocean the tops of the pines disappear in the mist and they're ready for their potlatch.

After the omming and The Big O they release one another's hands and light the candles. The Big O is what they call the energy circle where they join hands chanting till they get a strong current of feeling going around just like a cyclotron. Then flameshadows flickering on faces and the walls of the teepee each readies his offering. George begins by hacking off a tuft of beard with his knife and tossing it into the fire. After a while Helen takes off her kerchief. She looks at it a while balls it up and throws it on the fire. Blond Joan slowly stands up takes off her woven belt her ample body very straight she throws the belt on the fire. Paul takes off his headband and throws it on. Joan cracks one of her baroque worked mirrors and throws it on. Ralph throws in one of his socks Al laughs and throws in a long feather from his headband. Ron throws in a ball of paper

torn from his notebook Evelyn some fingernail clippings and
Dave last a lock of his brown hair. Quiet. Paul staring into
the fire sees colored lights looping up and down and in Joan's
wide eyes sees snow whirling and leaping like smoke as she
fingers her hair where she cut it. The sadness he feels is the
sadness of mourning as he stares into the fire. Evelyn's
cheeks are wet Ron sighs. It's the mourning of those who
have run away from home. It's the mourning of those who
have to run away from home as their parents ran away from
home. It's the mourning of those who escape the past who
escape into the present. Again and again. It's the mourning
of orphans in a country of orphans.

Evelyn stares at the hole at the top of the teepee where
the stars glimmer her voice flaring high and pure into a song
whose words are in a strange language Arab Basque Hungarian
its melody is flat stacatto with phrases that start in gutturals
and end in sobs flat howls of loss of grief out of some culture
much deeper than their own thin rituals and occasions much
older and irreparably lost. In the silence that follows Paul
starts tapping out a rhythm on his conga drums and Ron
next to Evelyn asks her Where's that from?
   Atlantis she says. Helen starts to meet Paul's rhythm with
her tambourine. Dave begins improvising on his guitar Evelyn
joins in with hers Al follows with his ukulele George comes
on with his harmonica dark Joan with her flute blond Joan
with her clarinet Ralph puffs at his altosax and Ron follows
along with jewsharp. After a while Paul begins to get into a
terrific beat against Helen's tambourine and he loves her.
Spike Jones plays the Rolling Stones he yells but the wine
goes round and now everybody's into it Joan the flute drops
her instrument and starts dancing Ralph gets up to dance
with her and Paul gets up to dance with them Al and blond
Joan are dancing off to one side and pretty soon everyone is
dancing except George on harmonica and Helen on tam-

bourine then they get up to dance but since there's no one left to play the music after a while they all stop and sink back to the ground pretty stoned and one by one start singing and playing again till no one can sit down any more and they're all up dancing and then there's no more music and they reel back to the ground each time Paul ends up dancing with Ralph and dark Joan and then just with Joan and he sees Al holding the other Joan with Dave smiling at them but Ralph isn't smiling at him but he can't get himself away from Joan. The last time they flop down she's between Paul and Ralph and Paul is thinking about Dakota about the long dark winters and the whirling snow and cold so bad a man can freeze to his horse and anything that happens happens inside inside where it's close and warm. And then everyone's leaving and when he gets back to his tent Al's sleeping bag is squirming like a spastic worm two tufts of blond sweeping the ground his dark hers the color of pampas grass. Through the night Paul keeps waking up to their hisses squeaks gurgles the bag jerking like a convulsive intestine. In the morning Joan says she's changed her name to Feather.

Hi Ron. How's the novel about us going says Paul.

I'm not writing it.

Why not.

It's like what happened to me as a comic. I used to be a comic.

I didn't know that.

You didn't know that. You didn't know that listen. You heard of Milton Berle.

Yeah.

You heard of Lenny Bruce.

Yeah.

You heard of Sammy Sax.

No.

Well I was Sammy Sax. I suppose you're gonna tell me you

didn't know that.

I didn't know that.

See I know what you're going to say I'm always a step ahead of you. It's all timing. That's all comedy is timing. By the way what time is it. No but joking aside I was very big very big. I thought you said joking aside somebody said that. So anyway there I was floating down the river on a marble slab. Oi vay.

Gee is this Ron I'm talking to.

Whaddya mean because I never crack a joke you think I'm a sadsack. Well I am a sadsack. That used to be my thing Sad Sammy Sax. I used to do an imitation of a guy about to get gassed in a concentration camp it used to crack them up. Too much.

Not sad I mean more like melancholy. Temperamental. Like Hamlet.

Listen Hamlet has some good lines. You could do worse he does some good numbers. But what do you want he has a good writer.

So why'd you quit.

Okay I'm playing Grossinger's see. This is the top all my life I want to play Grossinger's so I don't have top billing so what so they call me up the last minute I should fill in some schmuck broke his leg on the ski slope so what. It's my big chance. So I have them eating out of my hand right. I'm so sad everybody is cracking up I was never so terrific. I'm so good I want to be down in the audience so I can enjoy it myself. So that's what I do I walk off the stage and sit down in the audience. At first it's a gag right but all of a sudden what seems funny to me up there seems sad to me down here. Would you believe it I start crying I walk out of the room I'm bawling and they love it. They love it they think it's part of the act. Ridi Pagliacco. But I've had it. There are easier ways to commit suicide. Why do you think comedians are so sad it's because they're laughing themselves to death. So who needs it I decide to become a novelist.

So why did you stop writing the novel.

Life isn't up on the stage. It's out there in the audience. First I wanted to tell jokes about it. Then I wanted to write books about it. Now I just want to live it. After that who knows.

Ron is right. The unhappier he gets the funnier he is. The funnier he is the more he starts performing. He becomes a clown he makes a character out of himself a caricature. He invents stories about his own life alter-careers led by alter-egos. Some of these are amusing some even touching. They all avoid the one identity he can't invent. His own. That's why the more Ron loses his character the more he finds himself. The more he finds himself the less of a character he is the less a caricature. But it's not so easy to find yourself the self beneath the hard crust the hot magma beneath sudden eruptions of feelings the source the base on which everything rests. Not easy to find and impossible to escape. In contact with that soft core Ron experiences a numb terror which is first of all a terror of being soft. You have to be hard as hard as whatever it is that hurt you. You have to become what hurt you. Or else. Or else it may hurt you again. The recoil moves in the direction of character. Characterization. Caricature.

This is their first money crisis. Ron feels they ought to have a meeting about it but one of their rules is that they don't have any meetings. It's not a rule exactly it's just not the way they do things. So what they do is they get George and drive over to The River Queen. The River Queen people are allied with The Planet Krypton in their mutual difficulties with the Earthmen. The difference is that while The Planet Krypton is always getting victimized The River Queen mostly comes out on top because they have a lot of money and the reason why they have money is that they're big dealers which is why they have difficulties with the Earthmen to begin with. The River Queen people live on a big old ferry hulk docked in a lagoon on the river near a colony of houseboats. George knows their bosslady through Altair and Betelgeuse who deal with her. This is important because to The River Queen folks there are only two kinds of people. Friends and fuzz. The bosslady is a local character named

Fatima who is supposed to have made a fortune in flesh some
years back. She still deals a little in flesh on the side but
mainly now it's dope. When you work for Fatty as everyone
calls her you can pick up your pay in flesh dope or cash take
your choice. Fatty sweeps out to meet them in a long dress
a red bandanna and lots of big gold jewelry. An Everest of
flesh double chins double elbows every joint doubled and
dimpled with quivering fat when she hugs George hello he
actually disappears for a while. Fatty is hospitable passing
around some dope as they talk about work they're always
working on their boat over there and you can usually pick
up something to do. But two things make the boys nervous
one is the presence of Fatty's enormous Great Dane Prawn
with which she is said to copulate and it is true that it has a
funny look on its face for a dog even though she's a nice
lady. Oh well her friends always say to one another that's
her trip. The dog trip. Nice Prawnie give momma a kiss.
The other thing that makes them nervous is two bikers with
eyes like pickled onions who keep staring at them. Paul
remembers seeing them before.

It turns out the only thing Fatty has is some carpentry
work for George so he tells Ron and Paul to go on back and
he'll hitch home tonight. When George in fact doesn't come
back that night they figure he's stayed over at The River
Queen. Next morning George stumbles into the settlement
head crusted with blood eyes discolored one arm hanging
limp. Still spitting blood he tells them all he remembers
about getting a ride that drops him off at the other side of
the nearby woods about getting around three fourths of the
way through the woods about suddenly noticing an enormous footprint in the path and then another about five feet
on and a third after another five feet a sudden rushing in
the dark underbrush and that's all he knows. He thinks it was
a human footprint. He's missing one of his front teeth. The
money Fatty paid him he still has. When they go back of

course the footprints aren't there.

That night Paul hears the motorcycles cruising in the hills. Or is that something he makes up. Or is there some other noise or not so much a noise as the feeling of a noise that he calls motorcycles because he can't call it anything else.

Feather comes often now to Al's tent to make love. She still lives with Dave. Al and Dave are developing a kind of intimate comraderie Dave dark and bony Al blond and thick. The three of them together are quite charming. Sly jocular arm in arm. Generating a lot of energy. Just being around them makes everybody horny.

Feather has a sudden urge to hurry on with her big tapestry. She's been working on designs ever since the beginning of the settlement and now decides to start weaving even though nothing's been completely worked out. She sets up her loom in the area of the nearly completed house that will be her studio. The manycolored yarns are scattered in hanks about the loom. She's using ten different yarns for this piece and it's going to be enormous in fact she has no idea where it will end it's completely openended. This is because she feels completely openended due to her feverish sexual relations with Al and Dave. How does it feel to be making love with two people? It feels feverishly pleasant but a little unreal that is in her calmer moments Feather feels that it can't last though in other moments she wishes that it would. Well maybe it will after all in an eccentric time who can say what aberration or mutation will suddenly become the liveable norm. All these feelings and the need to make them coherent not to mention the sudden access of erotic energy are behind Feather's impulse to plunge ahead with her tapestry. She has all these feelings in her body and all these ideas about them in her head and she wants to bring the two together in the nonobjective patterns of her weaving but as the tapestry begins to take shape yarn after yarn she finds that the actual work gives her a tremendous pain in the neck. Of course it gives her a pain in the neck the neck is what's in between the head and the body.

Dave feels so changed by his new relation with Feather that he too changes his name. His new name is Goose. It has to do with this new feeling of risk he has in trusting Feather and Al so much. It's like he's really sticking his neck out but the more it sticks out the further he flies. What's so new to Goose is that oddly he's never had so much confidence in a woman before nor such sweetness in a relation with a man. When the guys kid him about his new name he barely notices he feels so nice.

George comes running out of the woods saying he's seen another footprint like the ones he saw before he got slugged but when they go back with him to see it it isn't there. Very strange.

Every now and then somebody in the area sees something black and huge sliding through the air. Something way up perfectly still sliding through the air black and so big it's impossible that it's alive yet it is. The ancient Condors live in the mountains to the east the biggest birds in the world bigger than their South American brothers there are possibly fifty of them left in these mountains and on the earth. Someone who has just seen one of these birds will grab you with pale face and glowing eyes without knowing exactly what he wants to say so what he says is I saw a Condor. What he really wants to say is something like I just saw a vision of universal death and eternal life but of course he doesn't believe in those things as tangible realities. If he doesn't know about Condors and the apparition came at dusk with the light not so good he might make something up to relieve himself Jeez I just saw this big damn thing floating through the sky it looked like a man with wings only bigger some kind of flying giant. There are wonders here. The brown snowpeaked mountains ancient empty shimmering with dreams through blankets of heathaze. Shapes materialize out of the misty pines in the morning and evening and at night with the surf throbbing and the breeze in the pines it's hard to distinguish what you hear from what you make up. The way Paul makes up motorcycles at night if in fact he's making that up. He feels a need to make things up to fill the emptiness to fill it with themselves their dreams and their nightmares the fantastic shape of their house.

For a long time Joan wanted to have a baby but she doesn't any more. Ralph and Joan are the only couple in the settlement who are legally married. She still has the same feeling of love for Ralph as always but lately she has a lot of other feelings. She feels she wants to do her work she wants to give her time to her work not to a baby and she doesn't want to give a baby her body or her whole

attention or her independence. She feels the strength of
the physical bond with her husband the sheer physical
bond of his touch and the touch of his body in bed every
night but she knows it's a bond she's going to break. She
doesn't think about it and she hasn't thought about it but
it's something that she knows. Just the way she knows
without thinking about it that since moving to the country
her capacities have in some way increased that she's capable
of things she wouldn't even have thought about before that
she has new energies at her disposal not so much a new
feeling of this or that as that she simply feels more. And
needs more to meet what she feels. For one thing she finds
she has time for everything takes an interest in everything
going on around her and gets an awful lot done so that
when she thinks back on her day she wonders how she had
time for all she did. It's not a matter of efficiency as when
she worked in an office but a kind of absorption in everything around her. And she works better than she ever has
before wherever she goes she finds materials for her mirrors
and constructions odds and ends of wood rusty metal bits
of glass stones broken shells things of no value that she
immediately puts to use in her pieces. This is why when
Paul comes on her making a pie of apples picked from their
trees he finds her crying. What's wrong?

Nothing it's just that I haven't thought of making this for
years.

So?

It's the only recipe my mother taught me. Don't you
think it's pathetic how little your parents can teach you? An
immense sky watery grey. On the horizon a mountainous
black thunderhead spits lightning at the wheatfields. The
house is painted white. The first floor is hidden beneath the
surface of the wheat but the second story and peaked roof
the silo can be seen from fifty miles away. The father comes
in big heavy-fisted too tired to speak no words to say what
he feels too numb to feel very much all this in Paul's head.
Did you live on a farm he asks.

Yes is suddenly all she feels like saying about it.

Ralph is driving down the highway in The Log Cabin thinking about potatoes when he sees someone wearing the intergalactic embroidery of The Planet Krypton hitching on the shoulder. The Log Cabin is what they call their truck since Al and Goose rebuilt it to look like a rolling log cabin including a chimney connected to the stove they use for cooking when they're away from the settlement. Besides the kitchen there's a family room and a bunk room in the attic so anyway Ralph pulls over and picks her up it's Cassiopeia who he recognizes because Paul brought her to the settlement once. Cassiopeia looks kind of beat and depressed Where've you been to Ralph asks her. Over at the River Queen she says.

What do you want with The River Queen Ralph doesn't dig the River Queen people much. They're too watery for him too fluxy maybe it's because Ralph is an agronomist or used to be now he does the vegetable garden and the fruit trees. Besides that they're okay with him except he thinks a lot of them are sex creeps and they tend to make him feel a little creepy. Like the way conversation turns indifferent and flat once they figure you don't want to get it on with them one way or another. And then he doesn't put down astrology Fatty is a ninth degree black belt astrologist they don't wipe their noses over there without consulting the stars and he's really kind of fond of Fatty you can't not like Fatty he just gets weary of the refrain What sign are you? What sign are you? If you really want to know I ran away from Krypton says Cassiopeia. How come?

Because Altair and Betelgeuse had a fight over me.

You don't mean they're jealous.

No we don't get jealous I don't know where their heads are at.

So how come you're going back.

I don't know Fatty talked me into turning a trick. It made me homesick.

Ralph goes back to thinking about potatoes. The reason Ralph is thinking about potatoes is that potatoes make him feel calm. Together. Rooted. And now he finds Cassiopeia disturbing. Her presence to him is like water rising behind a dam. Or a boulder on the edge of a cliff. An immense instability. Her slim body as she sits loosely on the seat next to him emanates blue throbs of sexuality that repel him and

attract him while at the same time he feels her on the verge
of some kind of emotional flood that could sweep the ground
from under his feet. And Ralph is right when Cassiopeia goes
into high tide there's no stopping her no containing her no
directing her nothing to do but hold on or get swept away.

Evelyn doesn't want anything to do with it. Screw it. If
Ron's going to start with his comic shtick she's had it she's
been there before. Okay she has no sense of humor she
doesn't want a sense of humor. She's only a nurse she doesn't
need a sense of humor. She feels the whole bit is based on
some kind of evasion and she thinks it's loathsome. Already
she feels Ron moving out of contact. Turning hard. Besides
she knows what it leads to for Ron after the Borscht Circuit
comes the sex trip if he's into a sex trip let him go over to
The River Queen not screw up her relations with Helen who
she likes. This is what Evelyn thinks but actually there's
more to it than that. Evelyn sees everything in terms of Ron
but that's only part of the picture. Ron is only venting what
everybody feels everybody is off balance waves of irritation
are sweeping through the settlement. The relation among
Feather Goose and Tom Al has changed his name to Tom is
making everybody horny and dissatisfied. There's been
so much fucking going on around this place that nobody can
get his work done any more and instead of satisfying them
it just makes everybody hornier. A new beat a new rhythm
is starting and nobody knows yet how they're going to answer
it nobody knows what kind of music it will make.

Helen rides into the clearing on her stallion Lawrence.
Helen makes money working as a part time groom on
neighboring ranches but that's not why she keeps a horse.
Helen has a horse at the settlement because she's always
had a horse and she works as a groom because she's always
worked as a groom. Even during her brief marriage. Just as
mailmen are now women so also brides are grooms she
muses amused again with the local cowboys' reaction to
her horning in on their work. Nothing like a horny cowboy
for the old male cock and bull. They can't make up their
minds whether to be nostalgic for the old wrangler or look
to the possibility of getting laid so they tend to lapse into
dull shitkicking hostility. Well like anything else it solves
some problems and raises others that's the way Helen thinks
about it. With George it works out all right he and Helen
meet like the king and queen of two different countries
allied but completely independent. Though George can ride
he isn't interested in the feel of a live animal between his
legs George rides the most powerful bike they build the
new Mitsubishi 1300 souped up chopped down and all set
to go to town. George is fascinated with the power of
machines and that's all right with Helen who thinks that
women are far more tuned in to animals anyway. She gets
down in front of The Monster and hitches Lawrence to one
of Joan's metal sculptures Ron is helping Tom and Goose
finish up the plumbing. I think she's just about ready to
take us in says Ron gesturing at The Monster.

I think of it as he.

Shehe then but I feel like we're about to move in to a
furnished womb speaking of wombs. He puts his arm around
her Ron likes to kid her this way she assumes it's kidding
Helen doesn't understand Ron at all but she likes him. How
about coming out into the woods with me.

You know I can't do that Ron this is my family Helen is
an orphan and it's true that she thinks of the settlement as
her family. You're my brother.

What about incest.

I've tried that.

How is it.

It's nice but it leads to complications.

Ron wants to know more but he can tell that Helen is in
her egg. He can tell by the absorbed expression on her face
and the way her eyes seem to look out at nothing. Going
Into the Egg is what they do to solve the problem of privacy
in the settlement with a lot of people living in close contact.
Imagine you're surrounded by a large transparent egg imagine
it with great intensity and if you imagine it hard enough it
becomes real. Try it it works.

They decide to have a ritual basketball game maybe
that'll clear the air. How is a ritual basketball game different
from a regular basketball game it isn't. It's just that they decide to call a basketball game a ritual basketball game when
they feel they need one and that in fact makes it different.
The men decide to call one when they feel there's something
to be cleared up among them even though they don't know
what it is especially when they don't know what it is. They
go back to the half court they have behind the house and
they choose sides by chance by coin toss. Then they just
attend carefully to what happens in the game with a kind of
split consciousness half in the game and half out of it like
simultaneous instant replay then later on each man tries to
put it back together in his head what they see with what
they do. It makes for a rather intense and stately game the
way people move when they're carrying too much to hold
on to. The sides are Tom Goose and George against Ralph
Ron and Paul. Twenty-four wins Tom passes in to George
he drives in to the baseline fakes a jump shot and passes
off to Goose under the backboard instead of shooting he
dribbles under the basket floats a pass high to the opposite
side of the court where Tom cutting out of nowhere takes
it for an easy lay up. George passes the ball in from mid-
court Ron steals it passes to Ralph who passes back to Ron
who dribbles once and stands still for a high archaic set shot
that can't possibly hit it swishes right in to a scattering of

stunned obscenities. George is easily both the tallest and the best player among them but he sees Tom and Goose working so well together he just passes off to them feinting and holding the ball over his head till he sees a possible play. As soon as Tom or Goose get the ball they lock into psychic contact with one another as they triangulate on the basket with impossible blind passes and unpredictable fastbreaking rhythms they make three consecutive baskets this way before their opponents can figure out what's happened. Then Ron gets hold of the ball again and without hesitation scores with another long high running two hander to general amazement. Everybody's amazed but Ron Ron knows he's in to a run that's what he calls it. When Ron is in to a run he can't do anything wrong it's this extraordinary thing that happens to him sometimes it can happen when he's playing ball or poker or betting on horses or when he's performing or writing even in social situations he doesn't know what it is or why it comes but he knows when it's happening it's a kind of power. Ron knows it but the others don't not until he gets his hands on the ball and makes another one of those long set shots almost without looking then Ralph and Paul start feeding him the ball every chance next time he gets it it's a long hook shot then a great floating jump shot from the corner then another long set he can't miss George starts charging him so he can't get off any more long ones he passes under him to Ralph who sends it back to Ron for an impossible left-handed hook shot next time it's a fastbreaking lay up meanwhile Tom and Goose still working beautifully together keep their side in the game. The score is eighteen — ten Ron gets off another hook shot while falling down George slaps himself on the forehead so hard he almost knocks himself out. Next time he gets the ball he fakes to Goose past Paul guarding him and goes up against Ron jumps for the lay up getting Ron in the chin with his shoulder Ron is down. They stop the play but Ron is only dazed next time George gets the ball he does the same thing getting Ron under the eye with his elbow missing the shot Ralph gets it off the board and dribbles to halfcourt the game goes on. But now there's this thing between Ron and George where Ron is angry and concentrating on George's drive in competition instead of being absorbed by the circle of the basket and it spoils his run when Ron makes a shot he knows it's not going to go in and it doesn't go in or if it goes in it rims around the basket and by some negative magic pops out again. George is getting every rebound off the backboard and now instead of making plays takes every shot himself hitting one after another and the score is even at twenty. But then something happens with Paul Paul is guarding George and he starts reading his mind sensing every move George makes an instant before he makes it so George starts feeding the ball to Tom and Goose but now they fumble around like a couple of clowns kicking the ball away or passing to Ron by mistake and nobody can make a basket. Everybody's taking shots they know won't hit making flashy pointless passes dribbling listlessly suddenly no one cares about the game there's no more fun in it. Ralph grabs the ball slams it against the ground starts peeling his clothes off yelling Time for a swim the others yelling stripping run after him down to the river-bank and naked leap madly into the water.

In the late afternoon after he's done with his work George often gets his board and goes surfing. If you ask George why he likes surfing so much he gets a thoughtful look on his face strokes his blond beard squints gazing into emptiness and after a while says Guess I just like it.

Here's what the women think about Feather having two lovers. Helen's seen everything she doesn't think about it. Besides she's done that Helen's done everything she knows how it is. Evelyn has her feet on the ground she thinks it's silly. She can't see it. Joan is curious. She disapproves. She wonders what it's like. She's jealous. It turns her on.

Here's one of Evelyn's exercises. First hold your finger in front of your nose and keep your eyes focussed on it. Then move your head from side to side keeping your eyes focussed on it. Then close your eyes while you move your head from side to side keeping your eyes focussed on it. Then take your finger away with your eyes closed while you move your head from side to side keeping your eyes focussed on it. Now open your eyes with the finger away while you move your head from side to side keeping your eyes focussed on it. Even though it isn't there. Or is it?

Hey says Ralph.
Hey is for horses says Joan.
Meaning what.
Meaning you know what my name is glares Joan. Ralph gazes back at her as if she were some kind of lunatic.
Don't look at me as if I'm a lunatic says Joan. I just wanted to know if you want to go for a walk says Ralph. It's plain to Ralph that Joan's got something against him lately but he can't find out what. At the same time she's become more and more demanding but he can't figure out what it is she wants. But this is precisely where Joan is at she feels like she has a grudge against Ralph but at bottom she doesn't really know for what nor does she know what it is she wants from him. Or even whether it's something he can give her. Ralph hopes

that moving from the cramped sometimes irritating confines
of the tent into the house will help the situation but it won't.
One look at Joan's sullen face and he can't help withdrawing
into silent anger himself. When Feather comes over to the
front of their tent where they're sitting on the ground these
are the vibes she picks up the dead look on Joan's face and
the stubborn hunched posture of Ralph's shoulders. Ordinarily
Ralph is shaped pretty much like a potato anyway but when
he's feeling good he radiates a kind of earthy warmth and
Joan can be as mobile as a poplar blowing in the wind. Without saying anything she sits down between them and grabs
each by the hand. Joan and Ralph incapable of any flow of
feeling between one another respond to Feather Ralph with
a guarded greeting Joan with a smile. This is what Tom and
Goose call Making the Sun Come Out she says.

How's the tapestry coming asks Ralph.

I think it's lovely but it's the hardest thing I've ever done.
That's why I came over here I have just a terrible pain in my
neck from working on it. Do you think one of you could rub
it a little?

Sure says Joan Feather lies down her face in Joan's lap
Joan suddenly all good nature massaging and smiling Here?
More to the side? Ralph goes over to the vegetable garden.

Ron is weeding along the row of celery. How's it going
asks Ralph.

Noi voh hunza schnecken.

What's that Chinese?

It's a patois. I learned it in Mexico. There's a small area on
the coast of Yucatan in the jungle where an alien tribe speaks
a language no one understands some people say they don't
understand it themselves. These people are dark but not
Indian no one knows where they came from or when they
got there. The local natives call them Turks. They work as
itinerant merchants and they run restaurants. They're also

famous for being good dentists. The Indians hate them because they're rich but they're also afraid of them because of
their language which is like a secret code and which they believe has magical properties. The Turks know this and play it
to the hilt. It's entirely possible that they just use this gibberish to impress the Indians and that actually their only real
language is Spanish they're real smart. When they start jabbering at one another you don't know whether they're laying
a curse on you or saying let's cut his balls off or just please
pass the salt. Anyway I picked up a few phrases when I was
there. Vash znagel p'tooi.

What's that mean?

I don't know.

They work down the row together. In his previous life
Ralph managed to crossbreed celery with endive producing
that very white variety of celery with the extralarge heart
that you're now just beginning to see in your supermarket.
Ralph calls it potato celery. That's the kind of celery they
grow in their garden. It's because of potato celery that Ralph
is able to contribute a small income to the settlement. Do
you know that celery originally comes from Iceland says
Ralph.

Really.

Yeah. It was brought from there to Europe. By the
Vikings.

The broadtails are running and George and Paul tack out
of the cove on *The Wave*. *The Wave* is the white sloop George
brought along from his previous life. The sea is calm except
for a gentle swell sky blue light wind blowing off the coast.
George handles the tiller and mainsheet Paul the jib outside
the cove they set a course downwind and take their clothes
off. Paul basks on the foredeck given up to the slapslush of
the bow cutting water the bob and heel of the boat the
radiance of the sun on his body. They're out after broadtail

and the whales are migrating along the coast. If they see a spout George will drop everything to chase it it's the kind of thing George likes to do. Paul worries a little about getting too close to one of those monsters there are stories of small boats being wrecked. George doesn't worry he never worries he just does Paul looks back at George his blue eyes sweeping the seascape. George has sky in his head thinks Paul.

It's not animals. Animals don't break windows and set fires. Or even slash tents. Every time it happens George looks carefully for footprints he never finds any. Once he goes off into the woods with his hunting rifle. Paul dreams motorcycle noise. Ralph is for building a fence but they can't decide.

They're ready to move into The Monster the way they do it is for a whole day everyone fasts and goes into his egg. The tents are down and everything is set for the potlatch which they hold that evening in the patio under the redwood around the fire. Everyone stays in his egg until they all join hands in the larger egg of The Big O. Ralph has a sense of imminence of new birth of a change beyond his doing. After all that's why you create a monster to do things you can't do. Isn't it? And then it does them to you. The omming and the energy go around when the egg is complete full of feeling and life then they break it. They break it with Evelyn's exercise Imagine a rose in front of your nose. Close your eyes keeping the rose in front of your nose. With your eyes closed see the color of the rose in front of your nose. With your eyes closed seeing its color smell the rose in front of your nose. Smelling the rose and seeing its color open your eyes and look at the rose in front of your nose. Take it in your left hand and pass it to your left taking in your right hand the one from the right holding the rose in front of your nose. Smell the smell and see the color of the rose in front of your nose. Smelling its smell and seeing its color make believe it isn't there the rose in front of your nose. Making believe it isn't there watch it disappear as you unimagine the rose in front of your nose. And now it isn't there what isn't there the rose in front of your nose.

To the accompaniment of Goose on the guitar Ron sings an interpretation of his song Famished crowbars rape the lute then they begin the ritual meal of venison stew baked squam wheat berry bread tomatoes cress and homemade peach ice-cream washed down with the sacral asparagus wine. And as they eat George begins to tell a story he knows from the local Indians some of them still live in the woods. It seems that in the time of the animals before men were created a god called Flows-with-the-streaming-clouds was lonely and wanted somebody to talk to. So he created animals who could talk and these animals were something like bears and something like men. They could talk but not through their mouths through their navels they used their mouths for other things like eating and fighting and reproduction. Also they couldn't talk about the kinds of things we talk about because their voices weren't connected with their brains they were connected with their bodies and instead of coming through the windpipe came through the intestines. So they could only talk about what they felt they couldn't talk about what they thought. It's not that they didn't have heads on their shoulders they did but they used them for other things be-sides thinking like seeing hearing smelling tasting and butting.

What they didn't have was necks. But then they didn't need
them because they didn't have any voice box. It's not as if
they were stupid they weren't stupid just different. Now
these Sasquatch as the Indians call them were very happy.
Their words were growls squeaks farts gargles clicks and
chuckles and they were always jabbering to one another.
They were something like bears who have just learned how
to play the piano. The only trouble was they couldn't learn
how to talk to the gods and this made Flows-with-the-
streaming-clouds very angry. So he sent the Condors after
them and the Condors carried them off by their navels and
shook them till their guts ripped and their heads were nearly
torn from their bodies and when the Condors were through
with them their voices came out their mouths and they were
men. And that's why men have necks because after the Condors they needed something to keep their heads connected
with their bodies. But though men were now able to learn the
speech of the gods they always remembered the pain that
gift caused them and they weren't happy. And so it turned
out that the gods didn't want to talk to them anyway because it was such a down. So Flows-with-the-streaming-
clouds ended up as lonely as he was to begin with. And the
Indians say there are still some Sasquatch left still hiding
from the Condors and sometimes they come out at night
but that they're very bitter after all that's happened. Anthro-
pologists consider this a very old myth that may actually
represent an unknown stage in the evolution from animal
to human that's why they like to dig around here. Some
inconceivably subhuman but superanimal species preceding
Pithecanthropus Erectus that might in fact have lived at the
same time as the Condors which are very ancient. Some
species intelligent enough to be free but too dumb to be un-
happy.

The Missing Lunk says Ron.

There's an awful lot of energy flowing through the potlatch this time Ralph wonders if anybody else can feel it.
Unstable energy roiling around making Ralph think of
thunderclouds. Feather sitting between him and Joan catches
both their hands and starts Making the Sun Come Out
though it seems to come out mostly between her and Joan
smiling at one another. Ralph starts thinking about potatoes.
Ron gets up. Though this settlement was originally my idea
as you know I've long since stopped being its creator he says.
Instead we all invent it as we live it. And in very real ways
it begins to invent us in return. And now as we move into
this big poppamomma that we've made I feel a change of
heart coming on.

For better or for worse asks Evelyn.

I don't know but a change. And I want to say that whatever happens from now on there isn't anybody here who I
don't like I won't use the word love because it's too crapped
up there isn't one of you motherfuckers or fathersuckers who
I don't like a lot. And because I feel this change coming on in
myself especially what I want to destroy in this potlatch is
my name for a name that's more appropriate to the way I
feel. And the way I feel is cloudy so from now on that's my
name. Cloud. Thank you brothers and sisters.

And then everybody starts changing names. Evelyn
changes to Eucalyptus because Cloud's changes make her
feel heavy and left behind. Paul becomes Wind because he
wants to change. Joan changes to Valley because she needs
a mask. Helen becomes Dawn because she feels like a new
kind of person. George changes to Lance and Ralph stays
Ralph because he feels stubborn. Then Tom Goose and
Feather change to Branch Bud and Blossom.

When Cassiopeia wanders into the settlement she can't
find any signs of activity though it's well toward noon so she
drifts on into The Monster. Half nude bodies are strewn on
mats on mattresses on the floor on pieces of furniture in
pairs and larger clumps. Under the redwood in the patio
Valley and Blossom are hugging and kissing. Bud and Branch
are off at the creek for a dip. Far out says Cassiopeia Valley
jumps up.

That's cool says Cassiopeia. What's going on here.

We had a potlatch last night says Blossom.

That musta bin some potlatch.

What happened was we all became brothers and sisters.
How are things at Krypton.

It's not Krypton any more they changed the name.

To what.

Golgotha they've all become jesus creeps. Last night Betelgeuse converted he was the last holdout. Him and me. We've
all been fighting about it for weeks.

So where does that leave you.

Out.

Where will you go.

I was thinking of heading over to The River Queen.

You don't think you'll go back.

Krypton's had it man. It's a dead planet. Jesus kills.

Nobody can be very exact about the potlatch it's all that
asparagus wine. Everyone remembers having a Pile. A Pile is
when they all crawl together in a heap on the floor everybody
hugging everybody else this is nothing new. What's new is
this time everybody is naked and everybody is supposed to
keep his eyes closed. After that everyone's version gets a
little murky. A big pulsing Pile of naked loving flesh everybody can agree on that. A lot of giggling. A lot of affection.
Suddenly quiet and a serious mood. Then for some people
it was sexy for some just affectionate a lot of people say it

was all anonymous but who knows who really kept his eyes closed and who was peeking. Two people were holding my tits one was a girl says Dawn. I was hugging a naked man I can't get over that says Wind. I know I fucked somebody says Blossom. It's like being babies says Eucalyptus. It made me feel so happy says Bud. They try to reconstruct it but it's like trying to reconstruct a snowstorm. The wind was in the eucalyptus. A branch was growing in the valley. A lance nipped a blossom in the bud and rosyfingered dawn burned through the clouds. And some time during the night a high wind swept through the valley and wandered sighing into the pines.

Ralph is getting a cold. He can feel it in his sinuses in his eyes in the onset of that general soggy lapse and leakage of energy that brings back the damp kleenex of early childhood. Ralph couldn't get himself to crawl into the Pile. The reason Ralph couldn't get himself to crawl into the Pile is not so much that he doesn't like Piles which he doesn't as that he can't get himself to close his eyes. He could get as far as undressing but he can't take his eyes off the writhing heap of flesh piling up in front of him. He's too fascinated. And too repelled. He has to see what's happening and so he can't close his eyes and let his body feel it. Whatever he does he wants to do with his eyes open. He wants to see things clearly. He wants to be clear headed and if he has to limit his experience to what's clear okay. They look like animals groping around in a heap. It upsets him animals are bestial he doesn't want to grope he doesn't want to crawl he doesn't want the ambiguous rewards of animality even with those he loves. Especially with those he loves. Carnality violence brutishness. And so his energy ebbs as he sits shivering naked in his corner trying to go back into his egg cut off from the animal energy of the group cut off from the energy of his own animal his body. Ralph has always been susceptible to colds since early

childhood and this morning as he walks through the vegetable garden shimmering in the sun he can really feel one
coming on. Still he doesn't regret his behavior last night because he knows he's right. And he is. Though now and then
like something seen out of the corner of the eye he has a
hint of fear that sometimes it may be wrong to be right. As
if there might be a larger accounting. And this uncertainty
much more than his feeling of isolation is a source of pain
to Ralph. That and the behavior of Joan. Or is he now supposed to call her Valley.

A visit from Buck. Buck comes over from The River Queen
to report arrival of a shipment of coke that's what he says.
But that's not why Buck comes over. Buck comes over because he's sensitized to erotic energy like a police dog to pot.
They say that Buck can tell whether anyone is fucking within a radius of half a mile just by sniffing the air. Or about to
fuck. Like water he tends to pools pools of sexual energy
that tend to collect in our geography here and there for whatever reason. The energy builds and builds till it can't be contained then the dam breaks and there's a flood. Sometimes
it's good sometimes it's bad it all depends. It can happen in a
household or a whole city but you can tell it's happening as
soon as you walk into the affected area. It's in the air in the
way people look at one another a kind of general horniness.
And that's why Buck is here. Buck used to be a minister
devout very chaste for years until his dam broke. Now all he
wants to do is get it on it's the center of his life his reason
for being his salvation. And he wants everybody else to get
it on. With everybody else. It's not only that he likes to fuck
no it's much more than that it's that he believes in fucking.
Fucking changes peoples' lives stops wars prevents cancer
makes you regular. He wants the whole country reorganized
into small towns based on sexual compatibility in fact there's
something small town about his whole mentality very apple

pie. Over at The River Queen Buck acts as something of an orgy master he calls it erotic facilitator. They say he has a permanent erection a real rifle barrel that goes off but never down. Get it on get it in get it off Cloud doesn't like him a cloud is always changing Buck always wants to do the same thing. Have some coke it hits the spot he says. The pause that refleshes as the Chinese fellow said.

We're not that much into drugs here says Cloud.

How about you he says to Cassiopeia. Come on over to our place it'll turn you on. You owe me a free one.

Fuck off Buck drifts over to Bud and Branch What'd he mean by that says Cloud.

Last time I was over at The River Queen Fatty talked me into turning a trick for him.

He paid you.

Buck likes to pay girls. That's one of the things he likes.

Cassiopeia doesn't like seeing Buck not because she once sold herself to him that doesn't matter. What matters is it reminds her of the way his flesh looks. It looks like dead matter as if it were laid on with a trowel. Cold as plastic. Dead. That's why he believes in trying everything it doesn't matter. He's never satisfied. Not by her anyway. S and M prostitution orgies whatever the squirmings of a snake trying to get away. From what. Its own skin maybe. And besides that his sperm was cold or is she making that up.

Valley blooms with Blossom Bud and Branch. Triangles
become quadrangles. Blossom's gotten it together she's
finished her tapestry. Cassiopeia seems to be staying. Quadrangles become hexagrams hexes are spells. Spells are magic
white or black. Wind and Valley are two points. He wants the
straightest line between them. Does she remember screwing
him during the potlatch or was it all asparagus wine. He
wants to talk to her. To say what. To break the spell. Prince
Charming. Vs. Prince Charnel. Enchanting. Will Wind sweep
away Valley. Shake Blossom. Blow Bud and Branch. No.
Sitting on the seacliff he ponders the surf pounds. The sand
takes the ocean's pulse. The sun goes down. The sun is huge
and orange. A flight of Pelicans glides across the sun. He's
in love. Another extraordinary sunset.

It's good they built the patio around the redwood tree. It
towers over The Monster and reminds him that there's a different scale. Larger than anything they can invent and against
which they are all measured. Not clapped together from the
fragments of their world but rooted in it and drawing strength
from it. The source of power the word behind words the sex
behind sex where he's afraid to go. And has to go. The
Ancien Caja. Schnotz. Vergimult. Bjorsq.

Dawn feels used. Just like she did when she made love
with her big brother. She still likes Cloud. It's just that he's
after something else not her. She'd like to forget about it.
And through the kind of mental amputation she's good at
she does.

As the tree invents itself each spring so Eucalyptus is
periodically assaulted by growth according to mysterious
cycles. In between she's dormant though flexible flexible
though rooted. She's a creative force good at inventing things
good at nurturing things that's why she's good for Cloud she
nourishes his imagination. She believes that if you imagine
something it can come into being now she wants to believe
the opposite that if you unimagine something it will not be.
She wants to unimagine the potlatch not that she wants to
forget about Wind Wind was nice that doesn't matter what
matters is Cloud and Dawn. There are some things that tap
a current of fear that runs deep beneath the ground she stands
on that can wash it away. She would rather unimagine those
things. Fear stunts her growth.

Lance feels good.

Is it possible for one person to love three people is it
possible for one person to love two people is it possible for
one person to love one person. Is it possible for two people
to love two people. And all at the same time. Things are
beautiful over at the quadrangle. Each night there's a kind
of ritual first two couples of opposite sex then two couples
of same sex then other two couples of opposite sex. Three
twos makes a hexagram a magic circle. Enchanting. Bud calls
their part of The Monster a womb. Branch says it's like being
babies. Everybody does everything to everybody. At the
same time. Sometimes they forget who is who sometimes
Blossom doesn't know who she is where she begins or where

she ends she likes it. She doesn't think of them as names she thinks of them as one flesh apart from the others the first legitimate children of the big poppamomma. Mutants. Monsterspawn. The natural offspring of synthetic parents. The children of Frankenstein. Other people's problems seem trivial to them they have the solution. They are the solution. Branch tells Bud they've rediscovered Eden Bud tells Branch he likes his snake. Branch tells Bud he's nice everything is nice even the snake is nice. Bud and Branch have a project the project is to perfect and manufacture a line of hip dolls that can piss shit and get it on a kind of anti-Barbie toy our values instead of theirs. It's going to be made of a plastic Bud knows about that can be pinched and palped like the real thing they'll call it Playflesh. They spend days on end working out the details Branch even writes to a toy distributor he knows who thinks they may have a real seller. The idea is to get some money in the bank. They're all getting along so well they think they might want to settle down together in their own house one day and that takes money. Even have kids together who knows they all seem to be getting into a new head. It's all dreams of course. Euphoria. Blossom has finished her beautiful tapestry no longer abstract it's a vibrant landscape at the end of it the sun sets. Now she's making tie-dye shirts. In three different patterns. She sends them to a store in the city. They're moving well.

Valley doesn't think much she's happy. When you're happy why think. She doesn't think she looks into her mirrors when she looks into her mirrors she looks beautiful she looks happy she finds that painful. Why. When she thinks what she thinks is that everything is horizontal nothing is vertical. She thinks that maybe vertical was always a mistake but sometimes she also thinks she wants to be alone. She thinks they're all like babies together she likes being like babies. She wonders what happens if she starts to grow up.

They're going through the seacave and along the cliffs to the next cove where they keep the boat. Ralph Lance Bud Branch. It's the only way to get there unless they want to go all the way around through the forest they're going out after flatfish. As Ralph steps out onto the narrow plank bridge they've made across the break in the cliff Lance sees one of the supports is down. He opens his mouth the plank tips Ralph is gone Watch out Lance yells. Ralph is on a crumbling shelf under the bridge gravel slipping beneath him. He looks surprised. He gropes for handholds on the incline as he slides the ocean washes the rocks a hundred fifty feet below he looks up his face looks like goodbye. He's about ten feet down without even saying anything Bud grabs a bridge support and holds out his arm Branch grabs his hand holds out his to Lance Branch and Lance lower themselves over the edge Bud holding on Quick he says Ralph sliding slowly looking stunned fingers scratching into the sandstone Branch works his way down Lance swings himself loose like an acrobat dangling from Branch's grip finds a handhold Grab my foot he yells Ralph finds it with one hand with two hands Brace yourself and climb can you climb says Lance. I can't it's my ankle Lance bracing with his hand slowly pulls his leg up Ralph scrambling grabs his hand hoists himself on Lance's shoulder up Branch's arm Lance helping to support the weight on his shoulder Branch and Lance pushing Ralph up over the lip of the crevice. Somebody pulled that support out look at that says Lance. He shows them. The nails are bent. They get Ralph back to the settlement Eucalyptus says it's a sprain she straps it up. Lance takes his rifle jumps on his Mitsubishi 1300 and guns toward the forest Where you going yells Bud.

Hunting.

They all run down to the beach and strip to their bathing suits for a swim. When they look around they discover Cassiopeia has stripped but she has no bathing suit. Everyone is cool. When they look at Cassiopeia their eyes make bathing suits there are little bikinis in their irises. Then little by little they're able to look at her without a bathing suit. They still put bathing suits on her when they talk to her. And when she plays frisbee. Though that gets impossible Cassiopeia has a lot of bounce full buttocks and breasts that flow like teardrops from her shoulders. Like avocados Ralph thinks. Like eggplants. There's a field of energy around Cassiopeia. Nobody pays special attention to her but she's the center of attention. Nobody talks about her but she's behind all the talk. Nobody moves toward her but they end up sitting around her. Nobody notes it but there's a lot more running and surfing and ballplaying and general animation. Next time they go down to the beach Dawn isn't wearing a bathing suit either. Dawn has a long lean body boyish with long full thighs. That's the way Cloud describes it to himself then he remembers that though he has felt it he's never seen it. Though he's been in it. It. Not has. Is. Dawn is a long lean body boyish etcetera. Dawn is not has. Cloud slips off his trunks. Cloud is a narrow body narrow and long mostly vertical. Then Lance takes off his suit Lance is a hard body muscular and flat flat belly. Then Eucalyptus Eucalyptus is soft rounded and bottom heavy. Blossom is thick in the waist with very large breasts a lot of pubic hair and a long thin neck. Branch is high shouldered and slim hipped. Valley is thin and voluptuous. Like a Modigliani thinks Wind. Wind is bony and too thin his skin is green. Bud is soft and chubby. Ralph is shirtless but wearing his levis and can't move around much because of his bad ankle. Ralph is feeling a little embarrassed to be the only one there with clothes on but his ankle hurts. You want me to help you off with your things says Cassiopeia. She unzips his pants and works them carefully down over his ankle. Then bending over him she straddles his legs Lift she says as he raises his buttocks she slides his underpants slowly down his legs so as not to hurt his ankle. Ralph is round and has a long penis.

Cassiopeia's dog Pulsar arrives from Golgotha sniffing his way into the settlement he trots in narrowing circles and breaks into a run as Cassiopeia comes around a curve of The Monster tail whirling like a propeller barking leaping high in the air practically knocking her down. Pulsar is a big Dalmation very noble looking and familiar at the settlement because of his obsession with picking up Dawn when she's out riding her stallion Lawrence and trotting home with her. Golgotha must be getting heavy says Cassiopeia.

Why Pulsar says Ralph.

Because pulsars are black spots in the cosmos that whirl around and give off tremendous amounts of energy. What are you staring at.

Nothing. Ralph gives his head a shake. It seems that Cassiopeia's head is surrounded by a flare of blue light but when he shakes his head it goes away.

They are worried about Ralph. Blossom brings it up with Bud at about the same time as Eucalyptus brings it up with Cloud at about the same time as Wind brings it up with Lance. Ralph hobbles around on his crutch from place to place in a restless way and also he does a lot of sitting and staring. He's been neglecting the vegetable garden and claims he sees strange lights which he refuses to talk about. In fact he refuses to talk about anything much at all. It's not Valley he's friendly to Valley except that he continues calling her Joan. It's obvious to everybody that he's going to sleep with Cassiopeia they wonder why he's holding off. His one interest seems to be in taking long aimless drives in The Log Cabin. Blossom asks him if he'd like to try Making the Sun Come Out but he says he doesn't want to make the sun come out. He goes around so obviously in a state of pain that everyone is getting very subdued out of consideration and empathy. Cloud thinks about it in terms of geology. Cloud thinks that we all have faults in our personalities but that usually they lie below the surface layers in the deep substructure until

some shift in the crust brings them out and we're shaken up.
Cloud thinks that this kind of fissure has opened up in
Ralph. The same kind of thing has happened to Cloud may
happen again. Maybe because of this Cloud can see that
beneath his depression Ralph is volcanic. Furious. Furious
not so much at Valley Cloud suspects but at the whole direction the settlement is taking and furious at himself for feeling
divided about it. Cloud can understand that if Ralph were to
sleep with Cassiopeia now it would involve an act of brutality.
Cloud can see why Ralph is depressed. One day he comes
back from a drive in The Log Cabin looking white and shaky.
What's wrong Cloud asks.

I saw a Condor.

What was it like.

It's a kind of vulture. After that Ralph spends more and
more time just sitting in The Log Cabin. Then one morning
they find him sleeping there and all four tires are flat. Why'd
you do that.

Things ought to stay in one place says Ralph.

Cloud begins noticing an odd thing for example one day
he sees an expression crossing Wind's face an expression of
pain peculiar to Ralph. Then another time he notices Eucalyptus' look of subliminal annoyance and he has to remind himself that he's talking to Valley. Once he catches Blossom
laughing just like Lance. After he notices this phenomenon
once or twice he begins seeing it all the time. Eucalyptus'
pensive look on Blossom's face Dawn glowing with excite-
ment like Branch his own smile on Dawn's lips. Bud and
Branch are practically twins by now. They're all becoming
composites of one another Cloud wonders what remains
unique to each. He thinks maybe it's a rhythm and maybe
a quality of response. The way he differs from his father for
example or his sister. He thinks maybe all the horizontal
things are interchangeable and the vertical ones unique so
that for example you might get people behaving the same

way again and again and always for different reasons. He thinks the vertical is like an elevator people go up and down according to temperament. As they go down people make some kind of choice about where they want to get off. The further down you go the fewer the stops and Cloud thinks that if you go down far enough there are no more stops at all and then you just keep going down and down and you can't stop. And then what. Bjorsq.

They're out on The Tongue. The Tongue is a spit of cliffs jutting out from the mainland from which you can see forty or fifty miles of beach and cliff in either direction. Over a thousand feet down the waves crawl onto the beach and the roar of forty miles of surf fills the air like rain. On the tip of The Tongue they can hear the bellowing of sea lions floating up on the wind mellowed by the distance almost like a song. Valley is telling Wind about her childhood. Of course it's not the way he imagined. It's true it was a farm but it was a depressed farm. Emotionally depressed. There seemed to be something unhealthy about it something off-color. Her mother was best described as a disappointed woman though over what it would be hard to say. Over everything. She died when the daughter was in her early teens leaving a heritage of thin soup. She seemed to lack some dimension that other people take for granted. During the dark snow-bound winters her father drank a lot. Neither were very sorry the mother was dead when she was alive he used to ignore her as much as possible. When Joan did something that irritated him the father used to spank her but the last time he tried she'd had her period. That was when she was thirteen. After that he would make advances to her now and then when drunk but never got anywhere and never remembered anything. At seventeen she was deflowered in what was essentially a rape. He was the highschool quarterback. She couldn't tell her father and didn't know what to do so out of loneliness went back to the quarterback who made her have sex with him again and eventually she got to like it. She left home to go to a teacher's college feeling she had been cheated. But of what. She never went back. She met Ralph while he was going to Ag school. He was kind to her when they made love and she didn't know what to make of it. At first she thought he was weird. Then she realized it wasn't him it was she who was weird weird and empty empty empty. She dropped out of school they got married when he finished his degree they went to Chicago where she began to paint she started sculpting after she saw Henry Moore's work the kind with holes where the vital parts should be. She never slept with anyone besides Ralph before the settlement except after the one time she had taken acid the trip had shaken her up but sex wasn't what she wanted she discovered. Then. She is very fond of Blossom Bud and Branch. Very. But she feels a little numb. Almost like a robot. What about you.

We were poor. Poor but high powered. There was always something going on. We lived in Coney Island and between the beach and the boardwalk and the honkytonk and the amusement parks there was always something to do. A kid had fifty adventures a day growing up there. But that wasn't all on top of that I was getting raised to be a genius. It didn't particularly matter what kind of genius though a great surgeon probably would have been preferable. My father was a failure and my mother had ideas. She scraped the money together for music lessons in case I happened to be a prodigy I wasn't. My father drifted from job to job while she thought big. What she thought about was a way out. I was the way out. I was going to be a genius. The trouble was I didn't want to be a genius. I just wanted to collect baseball cards like the rest of the kids. So I was stuck. I couldn't enjoy Coney Island and I couldn't get myself into being a genius it was too much for me I couldn't hold all that together I was only a kid. So I started screwing up I did badly in high school I kept running away from home instead of becoming a genius like my mother wanted I became a failure like my father was. It didn't go over big. I limped through a city college spending most of my time trying to reclaim the equivalent of Coney Island that's when I had a rock group. And then I got interested in politics and I went to law school and you know what happened. I became a genius the law review the whole bit. And was my mother happy. No. Poverty lawyer civil liberties civil rights no money and it kept getting me into trouble. I was the wrong kind of genius. Well screw that if what you are doesn't make them happy what you do isn't likely to. Then at a certain time I got completely fed up with politics. That was during The Dynasty of the Million Lies. Politicians are cannibals they eat one another to survive. I just don't have the stomach for it any more not now. Maybe another time. I guess I had some kind of break down. Or break up. Or break through. I had too much going on inside me the pressure was too much. I sort of broke open. I was kind of a bundle of parts that didn't go together any more. I need another way now. I need to put myself back together again. That's why I came out here. I love you. I've loved you for a long time I think. Making love with you the night of the potlatch was the greatest thing that ever happened to me.

That asparagus wine is very strong.

I know it but I wasn't drunk. You made me drunk. You're making me drunk again now. I want you to get out of that menage.

I can't do that. How can I do that.

Of course you can do it. All you have to do is do it.

What do you want from me. Do you want to make love with me again.

I want you to fall in love with me.

That's impossible. I'm already in love with Blossom Bud and Branch. How many people can I love. Or do you want to get in on it. I suppose if we're going to be four we can just as well be five but still there are limits. Don't you think there are limits. I don't know maybe there aren't. Maybe we could all live that way one big menage like animals. A menagerie. I don't know I still think there are limits. Somewhere. I mean otherwise everything gets all flattened out doesn't it. We were going to start a business. We were going to buy our own house. We were even going to raise a family together. Now I don't know what to think. Why shouldn't you be in on it. I like you too.

I don't want anybody else in on it. Just you and me.

You're crazy. What kind of weird scene are you thinking of. I mean I like you I really do and I liked making love to you that time I really did but try and be reasonable.

I don't want to be reasonable it doesn't get you anywhere.

You want me to betray Look he says be quiet. He grabs her hand. Just don't talk for a while okay. Just listen to the ocean and feel what you feel. Feel what you feel and feel what I feel. Why talk about it what good does talking do it just gets in the way.

She looks into his eyes. She looks away. After a while she looks back some veil has lifted in her eyes he knows he has her he can feel some magic starting to work. Something unreasonable. Something more powerful than reasons. I'm sorry she says after a while.

For what.

For being so stupid. I'm not stupid I just wanted to be stupid. Now I don't.

Why are you crying.

Because of Ralph because I can understand what this is doing to Ralph and there's nothing I can do about it. That's why I wanted to be stupid.

The Monarchs are back. Every fall they float in and flutter to one clump of trees here an old Eucalyptus grove. They cover it with their stained glass and it looks like seething black and orange flames or disturbed their flight looks like falling leaves. Nobody knows why they come to this particular grove. Cloud thinks they come like pilgrims to Palestine to their source. The Ancien Caja. The Missing Lunk. Bjorsq.

Ralph is neglecting the vegetable garden. Since Ralph is the only one in the settlement who knows anything about farming the vegetable garden isn't doing too well. If the vegetable garden doesn't do well the community will go broke. They're here because they have an idea first Cloud's idea then everybody's idea of Cloud's idea. But ideas aren't any good for vegetable gardens thinks Eucalyptus. The people in the settlement are committed to an idea but what gardens need are gardeners who are committed to vegetables. Their idea is to be self-sufficient. But peas and lettuce and carrots aren't self-sufficient. Only the weeds are self-sufficient and the weeds are choking out the vegetables. Eucalyptus has a special flower garden of her own where she talks to the flowers. She talks to them encouragingly as if they were children and the flowers thrive. Eucalyptus has always been able to talk to flowers she claims they need attention and respond to affection sometimes she even plays music to them. But these vegetables are different. When she goes to the vegetable garden and works among the wilted rows she tries as best she can. You can do it by yourself she murmurs to a nodding ear of corn but it's just talk. Mostly there's no response these vegetables are like orphans Eucalyptus thinks. Some do make it on their own but many die and many grow stunted wrinkled and deformed. When Eucalyptus goes to the vegetable garden now she starts feeling lonely and depressed and resentful after a while she just stops going.

Eucalyptus has always wanted to learn how to ride so finally one day Dawn gets Lawrence and they go into a field at the edge of the forest. Dawn helps her up onto the big blond stallion but once up Eucalyptus just sits there frozen It's too high she says. Dawn starts leading Lawrence through the field You have to get the feel of him she says. Don't think about being perched there on top of him. You're part of the horse you have to learn to think like the horse. You are the horse. But Eucalyptus doesn't feel like the horse. She feels

like she's sitting on top of all this power that she doesn't
know how to handle. She's not in control. And she doesn't
want to be in control. What's the sense of being astride all
this living power if it's just going to be another thing she
can control. When Dawn gives the horse a slap and lets it
canter off across the field she feels exhilarated and frightened
at the same time the horse begins to trot Rein in rein in the
way I showed you yells Dawn but Eucalyptus does nothing
the horse begins to gallop Rein in damn it pull the reins but
Eucalyptus can't do it the horse begins to run Dawn is running after them yelling and cursing You're going to kill yourself goddamit rein in but Eucalyptus is so evenly balanced
between fear and joy that she's paralyzed the horse begins to
settle into a hard run suddenly she jerks on the reins with all
her strength Lawrence goes up and back teeters on his hind
legs as Eucalyptus slides downs his flank and hits the ground
the horse pitches forward kicks out with its rear legs and
jumps off in confused circles. Dawn runs up grabs Eucalyptus
by the shoulder and rolls her over but it looks like she's just
stunned Are you in one piece Eucalyptus shakes her head in
confusion I'm all right You bitch that's the last time you
ride my horse Dawn runs off after Lawrence. Bud and Branch
run up to find Eucalyptus on her side in the grass shaking and
weeping quietly Dawn leading the horse back murmuring to
it You're lucky you didn't kill yourself say Bud and Branch
bending over her Take it easy you okay Why'd you do that
says Dawn. Eucalyptus shakes her head. Well don't do it
again she swings up on Lawrence. You've got to think like
the horse she repeats you've got to be the horse.

I don't want to be the horse Eucalyptus says all of a
sudden.

Well that's your hangup yells Dawn over her shoulder.

Maybe but there are a lot of things horses don't understand says Eucalyptus as Dawn rides off. The massive stallion
dwarfs her body as she settles into the big saddle. Can't
understand Eucalyptus adds. Won't understand.

Ralph has never liked dogs much before but Pulsar seems
special. He's been around animals a lot animals are cattle as
far as he's concerned another kind of produce he doesn't senti-
mentalize them like city people. But Pulsar's got some extra
spark there are animals and animals after all. It's not his
immense energy it's something else. They're on one of the
long walks they've been taking together Pulsar trotting along
next to Ralph dashing off into the bushes every now and then
stopping to wag his tail and point something out to him a
bird a dead animal a hidden clearing. The first thing Ralph
finds out about Pulsar is that he can understand how Ralph
feels he comes galloping up like a locomotive and if Ralph
is glum he quiets down even gets a kind of glum expression
on his face. Then as Ralph begins to respond to him Pulsar
slowly gets more expressive first wagging his tail a little then
rubbing up against Ralph to be petted maybe shoving his
nose into Ralph's palm then jumping around and barking a
little then dashing off excitedly into the bushes back and
forth back and forth till he gets Ralph to get up and take a
walk with him. Pulsar can communicate he can understand
the way Ralph's body feels he's more sensitive to the way
Ralph feels than most humans are than even Ralph is why
is that. No words to get in the way maybe no concepts. Then
Ralph finds he can learn a lot from Pulsar how to lie in the
sun and blink his eyes for example. How to stretch and yawn.
How to pay attention. How to concentrate with his eyes ears
and nose. How to nap when nothing's doing. How to accept
what he can't understand. How to howl at the moon.

It's one of those days one of those enchanted days that
justifies their idea. The sky is blue the air crisp and they
know they're right their only regret is that more people don't
see fit to get out of it once and for all and live this way. Some
kind of magic is at work everyone gets along so well they
don't even need to talk they communicate by empathy there

are days like this lately. People sing and whistle as they do their jobs hug one another even Ralph is working in the garden. A pink Cadillac bobs down the dirt road like a boat on a choppy sea and stops in the clearing the driver gets out a tall thin greying man in grey business suit and steel rimmed glasses. Everyone stops what he's doing the man looks around approaches Bud and Branch I'm looking for George he says. What for they say. I'm his father Hey it's Lance's father come on in Where's Lance at says Wind. Not Lance George says Lance's father I'm George's father.

You used to be George's father say Bud and Branch. Now you're Lance's father.

Oh really.

He's changed his name.

Oh really.

Who's here sings Blossom from the other end of The Monster.

Lance's father.

Lance has a father asks Blossom.

Lance comes in Hi he says.

Hello George thought I'd visit.

They call me Lance here.

Oh really.

Sit down.

I've been sitting in the car. So this is it.

Yes we built it.

Still doing carpenter's work.

That's what I am a carpenter. Lance introduces everybody just then Cassiopeia drifts through without any clothes on And this is Cassiopeia says Lance.

Oh really.

Can you stay for dinner.

No. He sits down. Lance sits down. Neither say anything for a while.

I hear the Lakers are winning says Lance.

Yes they're way ahead.

Again silence Lance's father drums on the arm of his chair. He looks around his lips pressed tight. Suddenly his mouth curls open Stupid he snarls.

You and your kind sneers Lance his face flushed.

Again silence. After a while Lance's father asks You need money.

You know I don't take money.

Still fighting the revolution.

Yes.

Responsibility Lance's father begins.

The hell with it says Lance. Dawn comes over This is Dawn my old lady.

Oh really.

Dawn sits down.

Mother says Lance.

You ask about your mother.

Ah shit.

There's a long silence. Finally Dawn says You're a lot alike. They both glare at her murderously. After a while Lance's father looks at his watch.

What time is it says Lance.

Time for you to get a hair cut.

It's people like you begins Lance.

I have to leave says Lance's father he gets up. Nice seeing you George. When are you coming home for a visit.

When they bury you.

Grow up George. You never did. Too much masturbation I suppose.

I'll come to piss on your grave.

Grow up son. That's all I ask. It's never too late. Lance's father trudges off to his car. Dawn takes Lance's hand it's shaking. You didn't have to say that.

Lance shrugs.

You are a lot alike.

Lance gets up and peers into one of Valley's mirrors. Then he picks up a candlestick and smashes the glass. Two three times. Till all the glass is gone and the mirror gives back nothing but opacity.

While it's true that Eucalyptus does not suffer from negative hallucination and therefore can see things that other people can't it's also true that sometimes she sees things that aren't really there in other words positive hallucination thinks Cloud. For everything you pay. Why are things always doubled in contradiction this way. Either way you choose you lose. It's always this or that when you need both Cloud is beginning to think there's something wrong with the whole culture. Body or soul. Dream or reality. Reason or feeling. Vision or sanity. Love or power. Eucalyptus' perceptions amount almost to clairvoyance yet at the same time she's afraid of what she sees a real Cassandra why is that. Is it because the order of what she sees threatens the order of our lives not least of her life. Eucalyptus is angry about his making love with Dawn at the potlatch You know it was just a special occasion says Cloud.

What's that got to do with it.

Well jesus everyone was making love with everyone we were all making love together it was like that German holiday Grinsing or whatever they call it.

You're not going to reduce us to the level of a lumpen orgy.

Well what about you and Wind for that matter.

That's different.

That's different. Why is that different.

That was just friendly passion. Dawn likes you. She likes you more than Lance.

That's ridiculous.

I know she's laughing behind my back.

Come off it.

I don't see why you want to humiliate me this way. Are you trying to drive me crazy or what.

My god I love you what do you want from me.

I don't know she says.

Well I don't know either.

What should we do.

Cloud sighs. Look it up in the *Whole Earth Catalog* he says.

Actually it's hard for Cloud to know what Dawn likes
and what she doesn't like. She was seduced by her brother
when she was a kid and she still likes him. He's okay she says
mildly. He's three years older they used to sleep in the same
room when they were little. Her mother was a drunk the kids
used to climb into one another's beds at night when they
were scared maybe it went on a little too long they put her
brother in a different room when he was twelve. But he went
on playing with her he used to set her on the freezer in the
basement and feel her up her mother was away in institu-
tions half the time her father didn't pay much attention.
They were alone a lot they used to get awfully excited finally
he deflowered her she was about thirteen it was on the
freezer. She didn't like it. After that he'd make her do it
she guessed it was kind of rape he threatened to tell the
father she was a slut sleeping around with all the boys. Then
of course she got to like it actually she says it was the best
thing that was happening to her around then her life was
really shitty at the time it was around when her mother was
permanently committed. She thought dates were stupid
she'd come home from the movies with some pimply jerk
who would try to kiss her goodnight and she could hardly
wait to kick him out and get it on with her brother. After
a while she stopped going out on dates to the point where
her father got worried and started trying to talk to her about
boys. Meantime there were whole days when she and her
brother would lie around the house balling they were some
of the happiest times of her life she tells Cloud. It went on
for about a year every now and then her brother would
make a resolution to stop like teenage boys with masturbation but he would always come back to her it was too good.
Dawn says she doesn't feel any guilt not that she's aware of
she thinks she's had more love in her family life than most
people she knows. After a while it just sort of petered out
her brother would ask her to ball one of his friends now and
then and she could usually dig it then she sort of fell in love
with one of them for a time she was sleeping with both him
and her brother the boy didn't know of course. Then her
brother found a steady and started urging her to date a lot

of boys he didn't think it was healthy for a girl going on
fifteen to be screwing her brother all the time he told her.
After that they would get it on occasionally in a friendly
way till her father died and they went off to different rela-
tives but mostly it was out of affection and nostalgia. Now
he's married and has three kids who she likes to go see but
she thinks she still wouldn't mind getting one off with him
except he's really straight now and tends to get a little un-
comfortable about the whole thing. Which she can understand because after all he did exploit the hell out of her
when she didn't know what she was doing but then he didn't
know much better and she didn't put him down. So if she
doesn't put her brother down for child rape what the hell
does she put down Cloud wonders. It's true she likes to put
down Lance she says Lance is basically a lunk but she likes
him too and she likes to make love with him. And it's true
she likes to screw but she can't have an orgasm unless her
arms are raised back over her head which means she can't
embrace him so Cloud ends up feeling like he's doing something to her that she's not doing back to him what do you
make of that.

Cloud is getting TV transmissions from the moon through
Eucalyptus' ass. There are astronauts up there and they're
sending back shots of the lunar landscape to Mission Control
Center in southern Frankenstein or wherever it is. Why Cloud
is getting the pictures through Eucalyptus' ass he can't say.
Maybe it's because there's no television set in the settlement
and the one thing he really wants to see is coverage of the
moonshot though that doesn't really explain much. Maybe
it's because the hemispheres of Eucalyptus's ass are a lot like
the moon. That could be because the transmission is coming
through the hemispheres not the hole. In any case Eucalyptus
says that's the nicest thing he's ever said to her. Then she
goes back to sleep. That's the nice thing about Eucalyptus
she takes things in stride. Some things. The dark side of

Eucalyptus is that there are some things she doesn't take in stride. Cloud is lying in bed with Eucalyptus pressed against her. The lunar landscape is grey-brown and soft edged as if it had been melted then covered with dust. Above the horizon the sky is black. All very barren but quite beautiful a nice place to get away from the clutter. As he was saying Eucalyptus has a dark side as well as a bright like the moon. The dark side you never see that's why it's dark you just know it's there from the things that pop out now and then. Like when someone is afraid of let's say brussels sprouts Eucalyptus acts like the rug is going to be yanked out from under her. Then she would be left spinning in midspace like the moon. Alone. When Eucalyptus was a kid her parents got divorced. She went to live with her mother. Then when her father remarried she went to live with her father and stepmother. Then when her father got divorced again she went to live with her mother and stepfather. When her mother and stepfather split she was old enough to go to college. Besides it didn't matter any more. Eucalyptus was already blasted into orbit. Her parents chipped in for the shrink but after three years she dropped psychoanalysis not because it did no good but because she didn't want to spend the rest of her life preparing for the rest of her life. She thought she would just forget about everything and do something practical and worthwhile so she dropped out of college and became a nurse but it just flattened everything out. Then she met Cloud and got involved in what he calls psychosynthesis and things got more interesting. Psycho-synthesis is the opposite of psychoanalysis but apart from that Cloud refuses to define it. Cloud feels that life is a lot like a novel you have to make it up. That's the point of psychosynthesis in his opinion to pick up the pieces and make something of them. Psychosynthesis is based on The Mosaic Law. The Mosaic Law is the law of mosaics a way of dealing with parts in the absence of wholes. Vat zen.

The children of Frankenstein are not psychological creatures they are creatures of biology and chance. First the parents create the children according to their dreams then the children create the parents in their image. The parents it turns out are probabilities of the cosmos acting through nature. They are not to blame in fact they are a lot like other children. This is a big relief all around. Bud and Branch have long since forgiven their parents. And forgotten them. They assume their existence somewhere in Frankenstein collected in retirement homes like aged orphans. In their place Bud and Branch postulate The Big Mother. The Big Mother exists because she has to exist. Bud and Branch know very little about The Big Mother but they speculate that she is fat. That she would give you whatever you want if she could. That she cares for you but in a casual way that is she cares for you but not about you. Anything but over-intense and very good-natured. Bud and Branch like to think of Blossom as a manifestation of The Big Mother. It's clear that Blossom is into a Big Mother trip. Indulgent but not obsessive. Her genius is to let things come and to let things go. Let things flow. She no longer has to filter events through the particular distortions of her psychology psychology was the trademark of a previous era. What we have instead of psychology is imagination. In any case psychology was always the science of imagination but as a medical science was obliged to treat it like a sickness. For Bud and Branch imagination is a cure what does it cure why itself of course. It cures psychology. Which is to say it cures nothing it's just a beginning but a beginning has one great advantage it allows us to proceed. Once we can proceed we see that there are degrees of imagination Bud and Branch talk about this a lot. Bud and Branch think they have just enough imagination they don't want too much imagination what for. Blossom has more imagination than they have but she needs it to get together what she's doing that's why she's into the Big Mother trip. Enough imagination to deal with your particular allotment of biology and chance that would be their standard if they were to imagine a standard. They think that Lance doesn't have enough imagination he has so little imagination they can't even tell where he's at. Where he's at is he has so little imagination he's completely at the mercy of what happens to him that's where Lance is at. Wind thinks that Lance is like a force of nature he thinks that's terrific but Cloud understands that a force of nature is simply the product of every other force of nature in The Great Computer In the Sky and Cloud thinks it far better to program than be programmed. The only way to program rather than be programmed in Cloud's opinion is to gather new data to expose oneself to the unknown to increase one's allotment of biology and chance. If The Great Computer is horizontal which it is then Cloud thinks it best to be vertical which he is with all the risks of verticality. Cloud feels that in Frankenstein the old programs are inadequate this is what he calls The Problem. Thus mutations become possibilities even though ninety-nine and nine-tenths of a hundred are doomed. Cloud thinks he may be a mutation. Bud and Branch think he may be crazy. They think he has too much imagination. What for. What for because through psychosynthesis Cloud can imagine Bud and Branch. He can imagine the whole settlement. He can imagine that they're all mutations but different mutations. He can imagine they're all doomed and he can imagine their different dooms. The only thing he can't imagine yet is himself. That cheers him up.

Cassiopeia no longer believes in nature. She is the first to make this claim and the others are skeptical of it. Things are cool between her and Blossom. Cassiopeia tells Blossom that Big Mother is a nature trip and she should come off it. She says it may be fun to play boy scouts and girl scouts for a while but that nature is already part of the intergalactic zoo of specimens that can no longer support themselves in the cosmic environment. She says that in a few decades nature will survive as an indulgence of nostalgic philanthropists in the form of special preserves within the global city. The only one who can relate to this is Ralph after all the whole trip of the settlement is a nature trip getting back to the earth or as Cloud insists on putting it getting back to earth.

But of all the settlers Ralph is the one who is closest to
nature close enough that he doesn't have to believe in it.
Besides which if he believed in anything he doesn't any
more. Ralph isn't bitter it's just that he feels like he sees
beyond everything especially beyond believing in things. It
used to be when he felt shaky all he had to do was think
about potatoes that doesn't work any more now he doesn't
want to think about potatoes. He stopped wanting to think
about potatoes the day he saw the Condor. Now when he's
shaky he thinks about the Condor and it makes him shakier.
So when Cassiopeia starts talking to him about the cosmic
flux now it almost makes sense to him. It almost makes
sense to him when she says that nature is just a fleeting
episode in the cosmic flux and that it will wash away along
with you along with me. It almost brings tears to his eyes to
be able to think of consciousness as a brief eddy in the
cosmic stream it's such a relief to let it go at that. So one
day Pulsar is going through his let's go for a walk routine
with Ralph when he finally rouses Ralph from his inertia
Pulsar leads him to the vegetable garden where Cassiopeia is
sunning nude in the broccoli patch and finally it happens.
Pulsar you pimp thinks Cassiopeia still she hasn't had a man
since she left Golgotha and it's no secret that Ralph is at-
tracted to her. Ralph would tell her later that it was the blue
glow around her head that finally broke his resistance that
he thought he could see a pulsing blue halo around her head
as she lay there. He also tells her that she comes like a tidal
wave and she explains how they used to work on perfecting
their orgasms at The Planet Krypton as it used to be called
orgasm is the closest we come to union with the cosmos
orgasm and meditation and death she'd have to teach him
how to do it. Then they did it again and after that a third
time and it's a fact that in the place where they did it the
broccoli grew bigger and bluer and tastier than in all the rest
of the broccoli patch.

Lance's first Search and Destroy Mission occurs when they wake up one morning to find the old teepee they had left standing cut down and ripped to shreds. He gets out his Mitsubishi 1300 picks up his rifle gets Dawn on the back of the big machine with hers and guns up the old logging road into the forest. There's a certain area of the wilderness he wants to check out he says and it will take overnight to do it. They leave the bike on the side of a dirt track in the middle of the forest and head off into the trees with backpacks. Lance won't tell Dawn exactly what he's looking for. Maybe he doesn't exactly know. Whatever it is they don't find it. When they get back to where they left the bike late next afternoon they find it smashed and burned. There are no clues except Lance thinks maybe he can make out one of the famous footprints he's always talking about though Dawn says she doesn't think it's a footprint or maybe she just can't see it. They hike back into the settlement two days late Lance still furious. Nobody's going to get away with trashing his bike he doesn't care who or what it is. Wind asks him if he has any idea who did it.

Whoever's doing all the rest of the shit says Lance.

Got any ideas.

Yeah I got some ideas.

You think it's those bikers.

Nope.

Who then.

I'll keep you posted says Lance.

A visit from Mr. Stamp. In the Deputy Sheriff's car. Mr. Stamp is not only the food stamp dispenser and the sanitation inspector he is also the Deputy Sheriff. Bud and Branch are shitting green because of their marijuana crop in the upper field but Bud and Branch can relax. It seems there are complaints in the town. The complaints in the town have to do with the Bikers and the Truckers. The Truckers live in rebuilt trucks and buses pickups remade to look like the Gingerbread House or Alice-in-Wonderland or Pioneer Homesteads fantastic pieces of Disneyland rolling around the landscape or converted schoolbuses painted like psychedelicized rainbows they travel in various loose caravans stopping here and there for unpredictable periods of time. The Bikers trip out in packs of varying sizes at unpredictable intervals. The Truckers believe that all property is held in common yours mine and theirs they will come and take a tool they may need without asking you but next time they are in the area they may drop off a hundred boxes of cat food they've picked up somewhere else which may come in handy if you happen to have a lot of cats. The Bikers have a different idea about property they believe that all property including women is theirs for the taking and they take it whenever they get the chance. In consequence of their conflicting philosophies the two groups have come into increasing conflict along the road and the resulting violence has inflamed the rednecks needless to say these groups aren't very popular to begin with. So Mr. Stamp has come to serve a warning to the settlement. About what. About possible reprisals that he might not be able to prevent.

Against who.

Against you.

Why us why not against them.

They're not around.

But that doesn't make any sense.

Maybe not but don't say I didn't warn you.

Cassiopeia has been missing her children something awful she gets Ralph to drive her over to Golgotha so she can see about them. Altair or Joseph as he is now called they discover that the Golgothans have taken new names all the men Joseph all the women Mary Joseph isn't there. So they put Lyra

Libra and Lepus into The Log Cabin and drive them back
to the settlement. There's just about enough time for an
emotional reunion between the three children and Pulsar
when Joseph arrives at the settlement. He drives up with
Joseph in a 1951 Ford pickup on each of whose greyish
rusting doors is painted in rough white lettering the words
JESUS CHRIST! Joseph formerly Altair jumps out of the
pickup and runs to Cassiopeia Whore of Babylon he says.
Where are the children. Luckily for Cassiopeia the children
are out of sight Cool it she says. Joseph formerly Betelgeuse
who is a big muscular bimbo moves up behind Joseph and
stands there breathing and opening and closing his big hands
like he's squeezing oranges.

If you think you're going to sneak the children away from
Jesus and raise them up in sin you're making a big mistake
baby says Joseph.

Come off it says Cassiopeia.

Those children are coming back to Jesus where are they.

Maybe they'll visit Jesus now and then if Jesus is nice
to them but right now they're staying with me.

You dare take His name in vain you spaced out slut. He
shall freak you out. He shall freak you out with His love.
Repent or else.

Heavy says Cassiopeia. You're really something else.

Our Lord wants those children and he shall get them.
Either now or he'll come and get them later baby.

Is that some kind of threat.

It so happens that Buck is visiting the settlement this
afternoon and he comes over in time for the end of this exchange. Come on over to The River Queen he tells Cassiopeia.
You won't have to worry about Jesus over there Fatty and
her friends will zap him soon as he walks up the gangplank.

Joseph glares at Buck. You shall perish he says.

Drop dead says Buck.

She's staying here says Ralph.

Who appointed you says Lance who comes up with some
of the others. Are you looking for trouble we're already in
enough trouble.

What trouble you mean the Truckers and the Bikers says
Cloud.

Truckers and Bikers hell who do you think is trying to
wreck this settlement.

Well who then Sasquatch.

You think that's so impossible says Lance Cloud can't stop himself from laughing. Lance looks at him as if he'll never forgive him and stalks off. What's with Lance says Dawn who's just walked up.

He's worried about The Missing Lunk says Cloud. What's eating him all he does lately is hunt and lie around. What is this a community or a permanent vacation he's starting to piss me.

Hell what's wrong with a vacation says Bud and Branch.

Nothing except a vacation can't last forever says Cloud.

Well maybe we all need a vacation from this vacation says Blossom.

You think we can go back now says Cloud.

No says Eucalyptus. Cloud and Eucalyptus look at one another. Then they both look from Buck to Joseph.

Well then where can we go says Cloud.

Eucalyptus gets up at dawn every morning to do her exercises. She does them in the patio under the redwood tree. The exercises are her own combination of Hatha Yoga T'ai Chi and meditation. She starts doing the exercises and then after a while the others straggle into the patio one by one rubbing their eyes open yawning and join her begin to follow what she is doing. After a while the whole settlement is gathered under the redwood tree doing the exercises with Eucalyptus. When they are done there is a feeling among them that the parts have become a whole. At least that was the way it used to be. Lately fewer and fewer people come. Yesterday only Dawn and Cloud came. Eucalyptus wonders whether today will be the first day nobody comes. She wonders whether the settlement is losing its charm. The way Eucalyptus uses the word charm it means several things. Eucalyptus believes in charms that is incantations spells. She believes she can charm people. She wears charms that

bring her luck. And in her good moments she feels she leads
a charmed life. This is not one of her good moments. She
has awakened with a feeling of dread. Everything is flattened
out there's no life in anything. No charm. A pile of tarpaulins
against the house is lethally inert. A rusting motor block near
it emanates death. Even the redwood looks ragged seedy.
Cheap. Cheapened by their settlement around it. Life is
cheap and death is cheap. She does her exercises mechanically.
For Eucalyptus the settlement was always an enchanted
place. If the enchantment goes out of it there's nothing left.
A collection of derelicts with a half baked idea. A colony of
demoralized orphans trying to give one another what none
of them have. Of course Wind and Valley are an exception.
The exception. Since Valley left Blossom Bud and Branch for
Wind they have seemed on a long honeymoon. They are completely apart. Yes and that's the trouble. But still. As Eucalyptus does the exercises things gain dimension. Her muscles
loosen her blood begins to flow. And Blossom Bud and
Branch are doing all right. Except that they seem to have
seceded from the rest of the settlement. Her breathing
deepens she begins to feel her center. And Ralph and Cassiopeia have something going. Finally. Though she doesn't
think Cassiopeia is going to last here. Then there's Dawn.
Dawn is always the same. That's the trouble she keeps
thinking there's more to Dawn but it never appears. Why
doesn't Cloud see that. She's afraid Cloud is moving out of
contact. Cloud and Lance. Out of contact but in different
directions. Dawn appears and starts to loosen up. Then
Lance. Then Cloud. Eucalyptus feels balanced. Things begin
to come alive. The tarpaulins are now harmless and the motor
block is merely inert. Blossom Bud and Branch appear for
once. Ralph and Cassiopeia. The redwood soars above them.
Another scale. Another measure. Then Wind and Valley
show up even Wind and Valley. Looking like they know
something special. They all move together. They all move
together. Together. Together. Together.

Cloud has tried up and he has tried out. Neither of them
works. Maybe nothing works. That's possible. They'll take
you part of the way but they won't take you where you
want to go. That's because you don't want to go there. He's
tried speeding up till he was going faster than anything else
but that was before The Ancien Caja. Since The Ancien
Caja speeding up seems like another form of skimming just
like everyone else. Cloud doesn't want to be a Skimmer.
Skimming is part of The Problem maybe it is The Problem
at least that's what he thinks now. For example Lance is a
Skimmer and Lance is part of The Problem. Lance is a big
part of The Problem. Part of the answer is The Missing Lunk
but The Missing Lunk raises questions and questions make
Lance nervous and being nervous makes him skim faster.
What Cloud is into now is slowing down. He thinks that for
him speeding up was always a way of slowing down. I mean
if you go fast enough you finally end up standing still capish.
But since you can't move fast enough for that Cloud now
thinks the only way to stop skimming is to slow down. The
best way to slow down is like an airplane when Cloud was
interested in up he liked airplanes. The way an airplane
slows down is it goes slower and slower and then it stalls.
After it stalls it finds itself vertical and goes into a nose-dive.
Down down down into the Subway. Down and in. The important thing is to keep going till the right stop. Assuming
there is a right stop. Fourteenth Street. Rèaumur-Sebastopol.
Elephant and Castle. Insurgentes. Bjorsq. Cloud knows something you don't know. Valley is pregnant.

Valley is pregnant. But by who is the question. Ralph.
Bud and Branch. Wind. Valley doesn't know. She can figure
out probabilities but then what are probabilities in view of
the improbabilities of a given sperm fertilizing a given egg
at a given time. Considering the odds only possibilities count.
Valley wants to have an abortion.

I don't know says Wind. Wind is upset. But thoughtful.

What do you mean you don't know. It's for you I want an abortion. I want your child says Valley.

I know says Wind. But I don't know.

You're against abortion.

No no.

Then what.

Then what is maybe it is my child. What then. And what if it isn't my child. It's your child. I love you. We'd be killing part of you.

Part of me I don't want.

If you don't want a child that's a different story. But I thought you wanted one.

Since I've been with you yes.

Well if you want a child maybe you shouldn't throw away what's given.

So you want me to have the baby.

I didn't say that I said maybe. I don't know.

See you can't make up your mind. Now you tell me to have the child. Very cool. Very altruistic. Then after it's born you start wondering who it looks like. You decide it doesn't look like you you'll take it out on me. You'll take it out on it. I want to have an abortion.

Take it out take it out what do you mean take it out. I won't take it out on anyone as long as I know it's yours.

Well if there's one thing I'm sure of.

No I mean of course it's yours says Wind. What I mean is since I love you I love it.

Very logical. But I don't know if your ego could take it. I mean. I don't know if any man's ego could take it.

My ego can take it. I think.

See see.

I'm just trying to be honest. Anyway that's not the real question. The real question is do you want to have it.

I think so. I mean if everything else was cool.

Like what.

Like if I could be sure it was yours. Like I don't want any connection with Ralph or Bud and Branch. Like I don't want them thinking they have their baby in me. Like maybe they'll get possessive. Or maybe they'll get pissed like who wants you to have my baby. Or you get sore at them. Or everybody gets sore at everybody including me oh I don't know it's a mess. I want an abortion.

All right have an abortion. I'll go talk to Dawn she knows a doctor. Is that what you want.

I don't know.

What do you mean you don't know.

I mean I don't want to have the baby but I don't want to have an abortion.

Valley. I love you. Have the baby.

Do you want it.

Do you.

What about Ralph Bud and Branch.

Since nobody knows whose it is we'll all love it. And you. It'll pull us all together says Wind.

What should we call it says Valley.

Whatever it is thinks Lance.

Blossom loves children. In a way she thinks of Bud and Branch as children there's something so boyish about them. She loves it when each of them is at one of her nipples that's really something else. That's part of the reason she volunteers to take care of Cassiopeia's children now and then. The other part is to make friends. She's out in the patio with Lyra Libra and Lepus it's a beautiful clear day sky deep air still sun warm. It's a beautiful day but under the perfect sky hell is breaking loose along the coast the surf even from the patio sounds like a cave of water collapsing a continuous avalanche the ground shakes when the breakers slam down against the

cliffs as if there were an air raid next door. Down in the
lagoon the beach is completely washed away and in the cove
on the other side of The Tongue *The Wave* is threatening to
break up on the rocks. And the ocean is calm except for
the shadows of a steady swell that moves smoothly in from
the horizon and approaching shore rises rises rippling foam-
ing curling rises crests crashes breaker on breaker on breaker.
They try to get through the sea cave to the cove but it's
filled with water now they're going around through the
forest to see what they can do about *The Wave*. Lyra Libra
and Lepus are girl girl boy. Five four one. Blossom thinks
they're irresistible. They are but not in the way Blossom
thinks. Lepus is crying. She changes his diaper he cries
louder. She gives him his bottle he knocks it away and
screams. She picks him up and rocks him he kicks and turns
purple. He seems angry angry at what. She doesn't know
what to do what she wants to do is cover her ears and get
out of there or maybe get angry herself. Lyra sticks her
fingers in her ears she starts yelling at the top of her voice
Shutupshutupshutupshutupshutup Lepus doesn't shut up.
Libra is sucking on a tube of glue Don't put that in your
mouth dear Libra takes it out of her mouth the top is off
Oh my god she's squeezing glue into her mouth she runs
over carrying Lepus knocks the tube away How much of
that did you eat open your mouth Nmn mnm says Libra
her mouth shut Blossom notices her lips smeared with drying
glue Oh christ her mouth is glued shut try to open your
mouth says Blossom. Mnm nmn mnm says Libra. Blossom
sets Lepus howling on the ground she tries to pry Libra's
lips apart with her fingers they don't open Mnm NMN mnm
says Libra I can't *believe* this says Blossom Shutupshutupshutupshutupshutup yells Lyra she runs around in circles
and falls down Blossom runs inside looking for first aid.
She races out with a can of kerosene Cassiopeia is walking
into the patio What's that for she says.
    Her mouth is glued shut.
    Her what. Libra come here. You want a lolly.
    Libra totters toward Cassiopeia. Want a lolly says Libra.
Cassiopeia laughs and wipes off her mouth I hope she
didn't swallow any of that the tube looks full. She picks
up the screaming baby Shutupshutupshutup yells Lyra.
SHUTUPSHUTUPSHUTUP yells Cassiopeia. Or we'll glue

your mouth shut she opens her shirt and sticks a tit in the baby's mouth.

Sorry says Blossom.

Good thing we're stronger than they are. Because they're smarter. *The Wave* is wrecked.

Where do you suppose that surf is coming from.

Nature says Cassiopeia.

Dawn is riding up the old logging road on her stallion Lawrence. She's worried about Lance. She's worried about Cloud. She's also worried about herself. She's worried about Lance because Lance has stopped paying attention to her. She's worried about Cloud because Cloud has started paying attention to her. It's true that Dawn is a superliberated woman on the other hand it's also true that she depends on Lance in a way to hold her together. At one time Dawn was a go-go dancer under the name of Dolly Dawn. Dolly Dawn was topless and bottomless. Dolly Dawn liked being Dolly Dawn. Dolly Dawn was so liberated she could exploit her own exploitation. She liked being a sex object. It really turned her on. It turned her on because it turned off something she really wanted to turn off. She wanted to be an object a thing. She wanted to be Dolly Dawn. It was sexy being Dolly Dawn Dolly Dawn felt like she was in rut all the time. Dolly Dawn slept with a lot of men in those days. She met them while she was working it was almost like being a prostitute. That's how she met Lance. But when she met Lance the thing that was turned off got turned back on that's when she quit being Dolly Dawn. Now that Lance has stopped paying attention to her she feels that thing turning off again. Lance has stopped paying attention to her because of his obsession with what Cloud calls The Missing Lunk. Dawn doesn't understand it and Lance can't explain it. He can't even say what it is or whether he's angry at it or afraid of it.

He's just out to get it. Whatever it is. As far as she's concerned it's a wild goose chase she sees Cloud ahead standing on the old redwood stump. She rides up to him he greets her with a bleak smile he swings up on the saddle behind her. She turns off into the forest. What about sisterhood she wonders.

It's not that Buck is in favor of mass murder don't misunderstand him. Or war. It's just that he believes these people are acting out the genetic script in which violence has its place as a safety mechanism against the overpopulation threatening the survival of the race. There's a kind of gut recognition of this state of affairs. People get nervous and restless they don't know why they mill around trying to find a direction like lemmings before the big plunge. Violence breaks out suddenly suddenly subsides finally becomes permanent and irreversible like rust while people talk about the imminence of peace. A thinning out is in the cards and the mass murderers may simply be those most sensitive to the thinning out vibes.

You think so says Eucalyptus. Eucalyptus is hitching back from town she gets a ride from Buck. Eucalyptus is scared. But not of Buck. Eucalyptus immediately realizes something is wrong. She can pick up on Cloud's vibes even though she's in town. Something is wrong she doesn't know what. She doesn't have to. She's scared. When Eucalyptus is scared she's like an amoeba the fear cuts her in two and she starts acting like the two halves are independent of one another. When they start doing that she stops being afraid. That's why she's listening so attentively to Buck. Buck fascinates her. When she's in this mood what fascinates Eucalyptus is what usually repels her and Buck usually repels her.

So don't put down death says Buck. We're all going to die you might as well give in to it. When you do there's an awful lot of power there. Death is very powerful it's the most powerful thing we know when you think about it. We get into that over at The River Queen. You ought to come over sometime.

Valley is starting to be pregnant enough for it to be obvious. The fact of her pregnancy has a curious effect on the settlement they all feel elated. Especially Blossom it's her idea to have a potlatch. This is the first life to be conceived here in a way it's the real beginning of the new way of life they're trying to invent she says. It's appropriate that they don't know who the father is they're all the parents of this baby they've all helped conceive it. This is a sign of affirmation and Valley's decision to bear the child is a declaration of faith in the settlement they ought to have a celebration. So they have a celebration. They break out the asparagus wine they go down the road for some homemade peach icecream they start baking squam and bubbling venison. Everybody is excited even Ralph is excited in fact Ralph is feverish. Ralph has been feverish ever since he started fucking Cassiopeia he's spent most of his time since then making love to her. Between times he practices the exercises Cassiopeia shows him for perfecting his orgasm so that when he isn't making love he's practicing making love. Maybe that explains some of the things he does during the potlatch that or the asparagus wine. First of all he gets drunk very fast. Then he seems completely hysterical keeps hugging and kissing everyone and singing Cloud's nonsensical songs over and over again at the top of his voice Famished crowbars rape the lute and especially The mare the scare the empty air.

> *The mare the scare the empty air*
> *The fire the ire the slobbering lyre*
> *The ox the knocks the final box*
> *The ocean the ocean the mama lotion.*

Then he announces he's changing his name. To what. To Quasar. Why Quasar because quasars are cosmic thingies that put out a lot of energy and nobody knows what they are. Then he zips open his fly and staggers around with his belly thrust forward and his wang sticking out. Then he tries to piss on Valley. Then he starts crawling around on all fours then he starts howling and finally they have to put him to bed. He falls asleep thinking about Condors.

They wake up one night smelling smoke it's about three AM the tool shed is on fire they run out with pails and extinguishers the sky is beginning to lighten over the mountains before they get it completely out. They manage to save some of the tools arson is of course suspected. That morning Lance talks the whole settlement into going out on a Search and Destroy Mission. He doesn't know what it is out there but whatever it is they better find it soon or it's going to be tee ess he says. He says everybody may have his own idea what it is but there's only one way to get it that is go after it. So they go after it. They get all the weapons in the settlement and fan out through the forest in squads as Lance calls them. There are three squads the leading squad is led by Lance and Pulsar and they move through the forest according to a plan worked out by Lance. At noon Lance lets them stop for a rest they've found nothing. A lot of them want to go back they forgot to bring something for lunch they're tired. Lance keeps them going Wind wants Valley to go back but she doesn't want to start copping out of things just because she's pregnant. They pick themselves up and beat their way through trees and brush till late afternoon. Nothing. Everybody's completely knocked out except Lance. As everyone else gets tired Lance gets more and more energetic eyes glittering shouting encouragement and directions he strikes off on little side expeditions on his own or with Pulsar once he goes all the way around the three squads comes back to them from the other side and is almost shot by Ralph before he has a chance to identify himself. Everybody's grumbling and cursing finally at the point of mutiny Lance agrees to go back. Just at that moment Wind looks up Look he yells they see something black and huge sliding through the air way up perfectly still sliding through the air then it's gone there's a shot. Lance is standing there with his rifle in the air. Jesus says Bud and Branch. A Condor says Wind. Nobody else says anything. When they get back to the settlement they find two of Eucalyptus's stained glass windows smashed.

Everybody has his own idea about what's doing it. Cloud's idea is that they have a group poltergeist. What this implies about the group isn't pleasant to think about. It implies there's a lot of loose energy generated in the group it implies that the form of the settlement is no longer adequate to contain its own energy. At the same time it implies an energy loss a hemorrhage. A deflation a flattening out. The significance of this is too urgent to ignore. Cloud decides to ignore it.

Wind takes Valley in to see Dr. Stamp. Dr. Stamp is Mr. Stamp's brother he's the local doctor. He takes Valley in to see Dr. Stamp because of the bleeding the bleeding begins in the evening after Lance's Search and Destroy Mission. According to Valley's pregnancy books occasional light bleeding is nothing serious but Wind wants to be on the safe side he keeps taking her temperature it's always ninety-eight

point six. Wind and Valley have gotten hold of a whole
bunch of pregnancy books. They're going into the whole
thing they've got it all worked out. They're going to have the
birth at the settlement everyone is going to help it's going to
be natural childbirth the farmer's wife down the road who is
a kind of midwife is going to do the delivery. Dr. Stamp
thinks it's all foolish but he's genial about it. It can't hurt he
says. It can't help but it can't hurt. Make yourself happy
that can help he'll look in on things he says. He doesn't
know if the bleeding comes from all that walking around in
the forest maybe it did maybe it didn't it's nothing serious
he says. Just stay in bed till it stops.

And if it doesn't stop.

Then stay in bed. Meanwhile Wind is reading *The Weekly
Log*. *The Weekly Log* is the only paper they can get in their
neck of the woods. One of their rules is that nobody in the
settlement subscribes to anything or has a radio or a television set it's not a rule that's just the way it is. They want
to be apart. They want to quarantine themselves. They want
to stay away from the general infection and give themselves
the chance to create something really healthy. They don't
even want to think about Frankenstein they want to create
their own thing what they want to create is an Antifrankenstein. The Antifrankenstein is going to be the salvation of
Frankenstein that's the only way to do it it's the last chance
they've thought about it. Anything born of Frankenstein is
of the nature of Frankenstein the only thing to do is stay
completely apart everything else has been tried it doesn't
work. Maybe nothing works that's a possibility. It's a
possibility they don't want to think about but Wind is thinking about it he's thinking about it because he sees from *The
Weekly Log* that The Slaughter has started again. The
Slaughter is the reason he got out of politics to begin with
he got out because there was nothing they could do about
The Slaughter. That was during The Dynasty of the Million
Lies when all they could do was fight over doing something
about The Slaughter. Now The Slaughter has started again
this time it's worse than before. Each time it starts it's worse
than before that's one of the worst things about it but this
time it's so bad it's revolting. Before he had the possibility of
its stopping to cheer him up even though it didn't stop.
This time it's so bad that even if it stops forever tomorrow

it will be permanently revolting. And what if it doesn't
stop. And what if it stops but goes on in some other form.
Wind wants to organize a demonstration but the thought of
a demonstration here in Stamperville is almost enough to
make him laugh. Wind wants to go back but he knows
there's nothing to go back to. He wants to go back but he
knows there's no point until our monster is bigger than their
monster. Or more terrible. That's a possibility.

    The whole problem according to Ralph is to establish
psychomagnetic contact between Venus and Mars. As a repre-
sentative of Earth Ralph has already made contact with each
of them but Venus and Mars are barely aware of one another's
existence and that's the trouble. Ralph is working on it. The
way he works on it is by making love to Cassiopeia. He makes
love to Cassiopeia in two ways which he calls cruel rage and
masochistic frenzy. These he abbreviates as CR and MF he
never knows ahead of time whether it's going to be CR or
MF but it's always one or the other exclusively. When it's CR
he knows he's in contact with Mars when it's MF he knows
he's in contact with Venus neither is the kind of contact he
wants. What he wants is something more like CMFR where
all the negatives negate themselves so that the positives can
posit themselves. Needless to say he is quite aware that
CMFR can also stand for Cassiopeia Makes Fun of Ralph
this is one of the main impediments to Mars-Venus or M-V
Contact. It's one hell of a situation and Ralph goes around
a lot of the time looking glum and pensive he confides to
Blossom that he is the first psychomagnetic interplanetary
diplomat and the burden is great. Blossom tells Cassiopeia
that she thinks Ralph is disturbed Cassiopeia tells Blossom
that Ralph is making the transition from Earthman to
cosmic consciousness which is a very heavy trip and of
course he's disturbed. She says that kind of cosmic trip is
necessary if you want to get it together because that's where

it's at. She also tells Blossom not to bother her because the moon is full and she can feel the tide rising. There's gonna be a lot of weird energy tearing around this place I can feel the dams breaking says Cassiopeia.

Valley is in bed. She has been in bed for several days the bleeding hasn't stopped. Sometimes it gets a little better on the other hand sometimes it gets a little worse. Her temperature continues normal. Valley wants an abortion. It's getting a little late to be thinking about an abortion I mean I don't even know if they'd do one now says Wind.

Right you would say that. You're the one who talked me into this in the first place.

I thought you wanted to have it.

I didn't want to have it. I never wanted to have it. You talked me into it you and your sentimental ideas about having children. Who needs more children there are too many of them in the world already there are so many they're starving to death they can't feed them all. So I have to bring another one into the world who needs it.

You said you wanted it you said you wanted to be a mother.

Don't try to tell me how I feel about it. I've already been brainwashed enough by you. What you're really saying is you want to be a father that would gratify your ego. Then I'll be the one who's stuck with it you can go off and do your thing and I'll never be able to do anything I'll be taking care of the baby. I won't have time for my work. I won't be able to go out. I'll be tired all the time. I'll lose my figure you'll start running after other women. Then you'll start telling me how I'm getting sour and bitter and next thing I know you'll take off with some eighteen-year-old and leave me with the kid on my hands. Fuck you I don't want it. Shit on motherhood it's just another way men have of breaking women. When's this bleeding going to stop.

Okay okay you want to have an abortion maybe it's still possible. I'll ask Eucalyptus she might know I'll ask Dawn she knows a doctor.

I don't want an abortion. It's dangerous to have an abortion now. Of course why should you care about that it's my body not yours that's typical. What do you have to do with it anyway who said you're the father. It's my baby not yours who needs you. All I need a man for is a stud anyone will do. After that forget it. The risks are mine the pain is mine and the baby is mine. Why don't you get the hell out of here and leave me alone. Wait a minute where are you going.

Out. Out of here out of the settlement and out of your life.

See see it's starting already. What did I tell you. I haven't even given birth yet and you're already running away. You're scared that's your problem. You're scared of me and you're scared of having a baby. Scared of women and scared of children another fine upstanding red blooded example of Frankenstein manhood. Well who the hell's supposed to take care of me while you're running away. Helpless in bed. Helpless. I get into a bad mood and you can't take it the first thing you want to do is run away. Pregnant women get into bad moods that's part of pregnancy and you can't take it. You react like a child. That's the last thing I need now is a child I'm already having a child. I need a grownup.

Well jesus you can't expect me to act like your father.

I don't want you to act like my father. I don't need a father. You know what I need.

What.

A mother.

Lance and his father are a lot alike I don't know how to explain it. They both have something extra that comes from something missing says Dawn. They're on the moss next to the high wispy waterfall where Cloud always goes when he goes into the forest. The fall runs down the cheek of a cliff about seventy feet up from there it drops in blowing curtains that patter into the pool next to them like rain or in dryer seasons like tears. Cloud doesn't know what he wants from this place. Or from Dawn. Or in general.

The way I get the picture he was very straight. A big jock in school an engineer interested in his father's lumber and mines. They broke when he was in college. He took a lot of acid and everything fell apart. He fought with his father over politics. Then over ecology. Then when he dropped out over lifestyle. For a couple of years he didn't do anything besides surf and take dope screw around. He'd deal a little when he needed money. Once he brought some stuff in from the middle east. But he's still a winner you know he still has that extra thing. When I met him he really had his head straightened out. Like he could really move in a straight line you know whatever he wanted he could just go and take it. Like he didn't have to bother worrying about a lot of zig-zaggy reasons for doing something or not doing something he would just move in a straight line and do it. Like he really threw a lot of garbage overboard and he didn't have to think about it any more. Lance doesn't think. He does. He's on top of it. But he's not happy.

Why sounds great.

Because it's just like his father. There's something missing. He's all flattened out I mean everything's so cool you'd think that everything's all the same jesus christ. The only thing that isn't cool is The Missing Lunk and that's crazy.

It's not crazy it's just part of the garbage he hasn't thrown overboard yet. When he gets rid of that he'll have it made. Only he won't.

Gets rid of what.

Gets rid of what everybody wants to get rid of. Gets rid of pain. Nothing matters. Nothing makes any difference. People are getting numb. It's the only way to handle it. I want to be numb. I want my friends to be numb. I want my girlfriend to be made of Playflesh. What's that.

What's what.

I thought I heard motorcycles.

I don't hear any motorcycles.

Listen. They're getting louder you don't hear them.

I don't hear a thing.

When the motorcycles rip down the old logging road into the settlement everybody freezes. A dozen decorticated deathtroopers storming out of a decade of B movies into your life. Unbelievable. Sloped back steering their jet propelled hunks of shiny plumbing at arm's length as if they're driving their own moustaches. This is all we need on the other hand what a relief everything's been such a drag lately everything is falling apart thinks Wind. Wind is falling apart he's a little hysterical. Tommy Angel bumps to a stop raises his hand the roar subsides he looks around settles on Lance. There's something wrong with his eyes they don't move. If he wants to look in another direction he has to turn his head You. Whatta you got here he says.

Got repeats Lance.

Got. Money booze dope women we want it.

I'll give you half says Lance.

Deal says Tommy he breaks into a giggle. Hey we wanna kill some Truckers seen any.

No why.

They run some of our guys off the road this morning outside Stamperville.

Hurt.

Nah. Killed a couple. You didn't see none.

A big one gets off his bike. Hey let's have a party I see a chick I know he says.

Is that Betelgeuse says Cassiopeia.

Hey Beetle Juice she's talkin aboutcha.

What are you doing with these guys says Cassiopeia.

Beetle Juice shrugs It's a way of handling it. Let's have a party.

Nice idea says Tommy. What about the Truckers bellows one of them. Tommy digs into his pocket pulls out a silver dollar You he says he throws it to Wind. Toss it. Heads

Truckers tails fuckers. Wind can't figure out what's going
on. The main thing he can't figure out is whether to take it
seriously or not. He intuits that if he takes it seriously it's
going to get serious and if he takes it as a joke it will stay a
joke. For five seconds he's tempted to make it serious. Drop
the Bomb. Clear the air. While he's thinking about it a knife
kicks into the dirt in front of his toe he looks up to see
Tommy throwing it.

Take your time says Tommy. You wanna hand me my
knife.

You heard him says Beetle Juice. Wind decides he better
not take it seriously. As he throws the coin up he invents
ways of taking it as a joke a shot explodes. From the other
side of the settlement a sound of hoofbeats a horse whinny-
ing as Dawn raises her rifle on a rearing Lawrence and fires
at the forest in the direction of the first shot Cloud hanging
on to her from behind. Tommy swings his arm and the bikes
take off in a dusty roar. Mr. Stamp's deputy sheriff car
bounces down the old logging road. He pulls up pistol drawn
What's them shots.

The Bikers yells Wind. The Deputy's car peels out ex-
ploding dirt and gravel.

What's going on says Cloud he tumbles down off Lawrence.
Before anyone can answer Noah's Ark rocks and yaws around
the bend drifts down into the clearing Noah's Ark is a
huge surplus amphibious vehicle done up like a number in a
children's zoo a skinny blond freak jumps out of the cabin
he holds up the flat of his hand like a Sioux. Love say we
need some things he says he looks around. Five or six freaks
three freak women and a crowd of freak children pile out of
the Ark. Like what says Lance.

Like that jack over there.

Like hell says Lance.

And we can use some fresh vegetables. Load it says the
freak.

Lance moves toward the advancing freaks. They pile three
huge cartons in front of him.

What's that.

Cat food.

Did you see the Bikers says Wind.

What Bikers.

They were just here.

Move out yells the driver they disappear into the Ark the driver slams the door sticks his head out the window We're leaving you the Baba. The truck pulls out jerks to a stop the freak's head reappears through the window Love he says they split when the dust clears the jack is gone the Baba is standing there a short slight fellow with a sweet smile and a shaved head dressed in white pajamas. Where do they get all that cat food says Buck.

Where'd you come from says Ralph.

I left my car up on the road and walked. Say did you want Joseph and Joseph taking those kids.

Where.

Saw them driving off as I parked says Buck Cassiopeia heads for The Log Cabin Ralph runs after her jumps in the driver's seat they head up the logging road.

What chaos. Cloud clutches his head. Cloud no longer believes any of this is happening. This is not real life. What was happening is now all over. It lacks credibility. Cloud is writing a novel again. It's almost finished.

What were you doing with Dawn.

What do you mean doing with Dawn I wasn't doing anything with Dawn.

You're lying.

Don't be paranoid.

I have reason to be paranoid when you're lying. Why can't you just tell me the truth.

It's none of your business.

You just want to hurt me.

You're hurting yourself what do you care what I do with Dawn. What I do with Dawn has nothing to do with what I do with you.

Stop playing games just tell me the truth.

I can't tell you the truth.

Why not.

You'll just get upset if I tell you the truth.

I knew it I knew it. Why do you have to do that for. I'm not good enough for you is Dawn so great. Is it such a big deal.

It wasn't a big deal but it was a lot of fun. It's got nothing to do with you.

What do you mean it's got nothing to do with me how can you be so sadistic. Why do you want to torture me.

Torture you. All I want is a little pleasure for myself that's all. It didn't mean anything. It was an accident.

An accident.

I mean it was pure circumstance. We happened to meet in the woods that's all. We were both feeling horny obviously there's been this sexual tension between us and we got turned on that's all.

It was all automatic you mean it was programmed by The Great Computer In the Sky.

I'm not saying that. I'm just saying that if we hadn't met at that particular place at that particular time in that particular mood it wouldn't have happened. But we did and it happened. That's all.

That's all. What are you some kind of robot. It didn't happen. You did it. That's the biggest cop out I ever heard that's absolutely schizophrenic.

Listen don't give me psychology. Who are you to give me psychology. You're as psychological as they come you're more of a robot than I am. You're just a different kind of robot you're a fear robot. I'd rather be a pleasure robot. I'm not trying to hurt you that's just my way of handling it. What I do with Dawn has nothing nothing nothing to do with the way I feel about you how many times do I have to tell you that it's just a question of time and place and circumstance. Why do you have to take it this way. Why do you have to make it so important it's crazy.

I don't care what it is that's the way I feel.

Well it's idiotic.

Is that it.

That's it.

The seal was there yesterday and the day before yesterday flopped on the rocks of the cove wide gaze fixed seaward. But today its neck is slumped on a height of rocks its head hangs down horribly whitened maybe from dehydration its ribs show as its breath wheezes in wheezes out already beginning to look like its own skeleton. Creamy bubbles of mucous inflate around its nostrils and drool onto the rocks in a whitish foam. Today its mate is there on guard a yard or so away watching and bellicose if Wind approaches too near. Yesterday finally it became clear that the thing was going to die. Today the question is how long can it go on. Anyone who thinks that animals have no souls only has to see this seal and its mate thinks Wind. The look of mournful resignation in the dying animal that of empty despair in its mate which every now and then heaves a sigh. Their sorrow and pain are simple and articulate. If only it would get better If only it would get better it's so simple If only it would get better. It's been going on now for a week and it's not getting better it's getting worse. According to Dr. Stamp there's nothing to do but wait. Nothing to do but wait and take her temperature and change the bloody sheets and give her his hand to hold when the cramps come. Eucalyptus is a help but seems terribly upset with her own problems he doesn't even want to know what they are. Dawn too seems disturbed. Blossom is willing but for some reason irritates Valley terribly. Cassiopeia hasn't been seen since she decided to stay at Golgatha for a few days to get things straightened out about the kids. Wind's feelings keep changing. First he feels sorry for Valley. Then he begins feeling sorry for the fetus. Which is curious he might as well feel sorry for a fish or for the seal for all the consciousness the thing has at this point thinks Wind. Yet he feels for it to the point of tears even as be begins to feel that after all it might be better if it were never born. The seal watches its mate helpless and heaves a sigh. This is a tableau that Wind is beginning to find intolerable especially in his present mood. Wind decides that if the thing is still on the rocks tomorrow he's going to come down with a rifle and put it out of his misery. It would be so easy. It would be so much easier on Wind. It's so much easier to put up with your own pain than with someone else's thinks Wind.

The Baba. The Baba isn't a dessert. He isn't a nursery rhyme. The Baba is a sage. They get a lot of sages going through the woods around Stamperville. There's a growing population of sages wandering from settlement to settlement spreading sageness like Johnny's appleseeds. Pretty soon wisdom will be one of the main products of the region. Of the nation. As Frankenstein as apple pie or squam. The wisdom explosion Cloud calls it. He says the growth of wisdom is due to people getting dumber and needing it more. Many of these wise men have studied in this or that discipline some have just got the call. The Baba is a member of the popular Faker cult. Only the fake is real. The power of the Faker cult was its emptiness. Everyone abhors a vacuum and so people whirl around the irresistible vortex of the cult and in their frenzy to fill its emptiness they get sucked in. The Fakers believed that beyond the bogus there is nothing the emptiness of the cosmos. Ralph can't agree more. There's nothing there nothing there at all besides the M-V Factor. Ralph wants to know what the Baba has to say about M-V Contact. He feels a rising. He explains this to the Baba. M-V Contact is degenerating. Also I feel a rising. A rising and a little bit sideways says Ralph. The Baba directs his little smile at Ralph. It is meaningless but there is no blame says the Baba. Try to see through it. Inhale through your left nostril. Then exhale through the right like this. Look at your finger without seeing it. Then see your finger without looking at it. No difference. Everything is foolish.

You don't understand this is urgent says Ralph. M-V Contact is fading. Out toward left center. There's a rising

and then after the rising there's going to be a falling. Straight
down. It's going to hurt.

No matter says the Baba.

It does. It's going to hurt. It's going to hurt a lot. I'm
afraid. It's going to be like Niagara Falls. Only black. And
very dirty. Then it's going to wash away and disappear. It's
going to disappear forever. I'm it.

Go to the source says the Baba. There's nothing there.
The source is emptiness.

Ralph shakes his fist under the Baba's nose. You don't
understand. It hurts he yells.

Blossom comes over. What's wrong.

It hurts says Ralph.

He doesn't understand says the Baba.

I understand. It still hurts says Ralph. He retreats to The
Monster gets a butcher knife from the kitchen heads for The
Log Cabin. Pulsar comes whining up he takes him along.
Over at Golgotha they tell him Cassiopeia's kidnapped Lyra
and gone with Buck over to the The River Queen. He gets back
in The Log Cabin heads for The River Queen.

As Cloud meanders back to the settlement from his walk
in the forest he hears a loud crack a bullet thuds into a pine
trunk above his head he dives behind the pine. Waits there
frozen for about ten minutes. Finally squirms on his belly
through the brush to the next pine down the path. And so
from pine to pine crawling crouching dashing makes his way
back to the settlement. What are you doing playing Cowboys
and Indians says Bud and Branch as they see Cloud zigzagging
into the clearing.

Somebody's shooting at me says Cloud.

Who says Lance.

How do I know maybe it's The Missing Lunk says Cloud.
Lance already has his rifle Let's go he says.

Where.

After him.

Don't be an asshole somebody's going to get hurt says Cloud.

Okay we don't need your chickenshit. You can't chickenshit out of this or somebody'll be taking a potshot at us every time we walk in or out of the settlement we'll have to move in armed convoys. What do you say he says to Bud and Branch.

Well says Bud.

Okay says Branch.

They head off into the bushes. Lance looks around as they go Up yours he says.

You too says Cloud. Cloud drifts across the clearing. It's been overcast all day and as he approaches The Monster it begins to rain lightly. This seems to encourage a certain Mockingbird which gets into a duet with its mate. Bjorsq bjorsq says one. Bjorsqi bjorsqi bjorsqi answers the other. Cloud meets the Baba in the patio under the redwood tree the Baba flashes his little smile. Eucalyptus is sleeping with someone he tells the Baba.

Oh. No matter.

Yeah. I think it's Lance.

No blame no blame.

Yeah. What should I do.

Make yourself empty says the Baba.

Baba says Cloud.

Yes.

Baba Baba. Baba Baba Baba. Baba Baba Baba Baba. Bjorsq. When is supper says the Baba.

Eucalyptus is sleeping with someone but it's not Lance. It's Buck. And she likes it. She likes it a lot especially today. Today Buck turns her on with cocaine for the first time Eucalyptus can't get enough. She knows she'll do it again if she gets the chance. When Buck asks her to ball his friends she says no but she knows she'd do that too. Buck wants

her to try it on acid. He wants her to do his whole trip.
She knows what he's trying to do to her. She knows it's a
death trip and she digs it she can always get out when she's
had enough. When she gets back to their space Cloud is
there. She wants to get it on with him but he's indifferent
Cloud knows she's been with someone it leaves him cold.
Cloud is indifferent about everything lately. Indifferent and
nonsensical. Baba Baba Baba he says when she rubs against
him. Baba Baba Baba Bjorsq.

The River Queen is the name of Fatty's old stern-wheeler.
It's also the name of the community of houseboats rafts and
barges moored around it all connected to one another a
crowded labyrinthine village of floating freaks. As Ralph
steps on board The River Queen he catches a glimpse of
Cassiopeia two barges down. He waves and heads over that
way Pulsar bounding on ahead but immediately finds himself at the edge of a houseboat looking over an empty
channel to the next barge. He goes the length of the boat
he's on and climbs down to a large empty raft at the stern
continues on down the raft still without a way of crossing
the channel. He runs across another houseboat climbs over
onto a barge moored alongside doubles back along the
other side of the channel finds himself cut off by still
another channel jumps over onto another boat finally
reaches the boat where he thought he saw Cassiopeia. Of
course she's not there. Or maybe Ralph's not there maybe
it's the wrong boat Ralph can't tell. Meanwhile dogs are
barking at him the residents are staring with hostile sus-
picious looks. The people here are freaks but they're very
hard mean looking freaks. The men look tough the women
ratty and strung out except for a few girls he notices who
look overdressed for the scene like models or actresses or
rich girls slumming or whoring or scoring something or other
maybe sex. Or maybe just dope. Or maybe some other kind
of thrill. A muscular blond long hair steps out of a cabin

comes up close gives him a hard empty look. Peace brother what's your scene he says.

Have you seen Cassiopeia Ralph says.

Cassy who.

I'm looking for a girl named Cassiopeia have you seen her.

Never heard of the chick. Way out's over that way. Ralph heads over that way. The freak stands there watching him till he's out of sight. But Ralph can't find the way out he keeps climbing over boats barges up ladders across railings Pulsar always rotating around somewhere Ralph mumbling muttering at people who challenge him. Finally two big freaks grab him by the elbows and lead him back over to The River Queen. What are you some kind of fuzz says one.

Nah he's just freaked out says the other.

What do you want says the first.

M-V says Ralph.

M-V says the second I never heard of that one.

Sure it's that animal tranquilizer that's been going around says the other. Fatty comes out to see what's going on she hardly has a chance to say Cassiopeia isn't here when Ralph breaks away from the two freaks and pulls his butcher knife on her. Fatty's huge Great Dane Prawn leaps out of nowhere and jumps snarling for Ralph's throat he's intercepted in midair by a white streak that knocks him to one side the two dogs fall to the deck in a snarling ball of tails and teeth. It's over immediately Ralph held down on the deck by the two freaks Fatty calling snarling Prawn to heel Pulsar dwarfed by the Great Dane yelping and running in circles his bleeding balls hanging by a piece of skin the blood is thinned on the deck by a light rain that starts to fall We'll have to get a vet to finish that job says one of the freaks. What about this nut.

Call Stamp says Fatty. They take Ralph away in the back seat of the Deputy Sheriff's car muttering to himself behind the grating.

Buck stamps in through the wet. The rain is getting
heavier. What the hell is going on around here he shakes
himself off. Somebody just put a shot through my rear
window. Nobody gets very excited. Cloud shrugs his
shoulders. Sonofabitch mutters Lance.

Well aren't you going to do anything about it I mean
doesn't this interest you says Buck.

What should we do says Wind. They don't know what
to do about it. Almost everybody gets shot at lately as
they come into the settlement. Sometimes they come and
go in armed groups but mostly they just watch themselves.
After all nobody's been hurt yet. It's standard procedure.
If they wanted to kill somebody they would've by now.
Maybe they've got a permit says Cloud.

We've been posting sentries. Now and then we go out
on an S & D. But we haven't found anything says Lance.

What's an S & D.

Search and Destroy. On top of that the vegetable garden's
been torn up. Looks like some animal. Some big animal.

How long can you guys hold out says Buck. He sits
down at the table.

Fuck you says Lance.

Help yourself. You been around so much lately you
might as well move in says Cloud. He's like a vulture thinks
Cloud he smells the end. He wants to see what he can pick
up.

How's Valley still bleeding says Buck.

Nobody answers. Valley has been bleeding clots for the
last two days redgrey clumps of coagulated matter. The
cramps come more often. Dr. Stamp says nothing to do but
wait. Wind waits. He doesn't get much sleep. He does what
he can to make her feel better which is nothing. He holds
her hand he brings food to the room he changes the bloody
sheets he takes her temperature it's always normal. Now she
doesn't want to lose the child. Now when it seems obvious
it would be better if she miscarried she hangs on desperately
it must be hormones. It might be defective it might be a
monster. Wind doesn't dare tell her to let it go. He feels
like it's been raining blood for two weeks. Wind waits he
hopes it's over soon.

Heard of a job the redneck bar needs a bottomless dancer
says Buck. Thought Dawn might be interested.

Why'n hell you think I might be interested says Dawn.

Why don't you try it we could use the bread says Lance.

Dawn doesn't even say anything she just picks up her glass and throws it at him. Followed by her plate. That's it. That's all. You bastard. I'm getting out she stutters.

Calm down says Lance. He's picking food off his clothes.

Calm down. Fuck. She throws her fork at him. You're not a man you're a wooden Indian. You too she yells at Cloud. All of you all of you. She jumps up she tips the dinner table over she starts throwing things at the walls yelling and cursing. Nobody knows what to do. Eucalyptus always thought there must be more to Dawn than showed here it is she flashes. Buck grabs Dawn and pins her arms Take it easy take it easy. Soon as he gets a firm hold she stops struggling but keeps on yelling and cursing. The Baba comes over and starts squeezing and rubbing the back of her neck. That seems to calm her down. Suddenly she starts crying. That's right empty yourself. No difference no blame he murmurs Let her go. He puts his arm around her shoulders runs his hand down her spine back up to her neck squeezing carressing down to her buttocks he walks her off toward one of the rooms hand on her buttocks It's all right leave her to me he says. They leave her to him.

She wakes him up in the middle of the night she's having terrible cramps doubled over white. She's bleeding heavily he gets her into the bathroom. Clots as big as your fist are coming out. He calls Dr. Stamp get her to the hospital he says. The hospital is in town not Stamperville but the county seat fifty miles away. Ralph is out somewhere with The Log Cabin. Valley looks like she's about to faint he calls Eucalyptus and races through the rain to the farm down the road. He wakes up the farmer and borrows his pickup they get Valley into the pickup on a pile of towels. The cramps have eased but the blood is soaking through. He drives as fast as he can but the rain is heavy before he gets her to the hospital she passes out. The towels are full of blood it's

already light by the time they arrive. The first thing they
do is give her a transfusion. She'll be all right the doctor
tells him but we're going to have to go in there for a D & C.
What's a D & C.
To make sure there's nothing left.
Oh. Another Search and Destroy Mission thinks Wind.

It's raining. It rained all night. It was raining yesterday and
the day before yesterday and the day before. It's raining
today and it's getting heavier vertical black rain from grey
stationary clouds. The water pools in mudholes earth turns
to mud streams and rivers boil brown and white. They wake
up in the morning to find the patio half filled with a foot
of ooze washed down from the dirt cliff behind The Monster.
Jesus Christ! comes skidding down the logging road with
Joseph and Cassiopeia inside Pulsar riding in the truck bed.
Love says Joseph. Mary's here to pick up her things. She
wants to come back to Jesus. Cloud goes into The Monster
to give her a hand. How come says Cloud.
What's the alternative. Buck offered to get back the other
kids and keep Golgotha off. If he could pimp for me. I don't
find that as thrilling as he does. She shrugs. Mary Joseph
yells from the patio.
Why don't you guys come over there's plenty of room at
Golgotha says Joseph. Pulsar keeps sitting down to lick his
balls. They aren't there. He keeps looking up at Cassiopeia
for an explanation.
Come on Mary says Joseph he steers her back to Jesus
Christ! The pickup goes sliding back up the road.

The last S & D Mission. The last S & D Mission takes place after Eucalyptus has moved to The River Queen with Buck. After Ralph is released in Valley's custody on condition he get out of the area immediately. After Dawn takes the bottomless job at the redneck bar on the advice of the Baba who moves in with her in Stamperville. It's raining of course though it's let up some it's more like a thick floating drizzle. Blossom Bud and Branch are there. Wind and Cloud. And Lance. Cloud goes along because he goes along with everything now. Goes along blows along. Blows along flows along. A stick on the stream a wick on the steam a crick on the scheme. Wuzza wuzza. Schlunk.

This time Lance has a plaster cast. Nobody's seen the footprint naturally but everybody's seen the plaster cast. It's very indistinct hard to tell if it's a footprint at all about twice the size of a man's but it resembles a man's except for what looks like a cleft down the center. Not kosher observes Cloud.

This is what's been causing all our trouble says Lance waving the cast around.

The filthy schmutz says Cloud. They sludge through the soggy forest.

So you're going back to the city says Bud and Branch.

Looks like. Valley says she feels responsible for Ralph now. She wants to stick with him it's either that or the state bug house besides she's pretty shaky herself she just sits and stares. Anyway The Slaughter is getting on my nerves again. There's nothing you can do about it up here you know. So I'm going back it won't do any good of course says Wind.

Don't you care at all about Dawn going over to the redneck bar says Blossom.

It's where I found her says Lance.

But I mean don't you care at all.

Everybody's on his own. Keep your eyes open.

There it is there it is yells Cloud.

What what.

The Missing Lunk. Lance swings his rifle around wildly. I don't see it.

I didn't see it I heard it. I heard it come out of your mouth.

What's he talking about says Lance.

Do you think intelligent life exists on earth says Cloud.

Someone shut this fool's mouth. Come on we've got a

lot of ground to cover. Lance looks at his maps. Lance now
has government survey maps of the whole area. He's got
all the regions sectioned off. They head for the old logging
road to cross over from section D to section B2. When they
reach the road they sight the Ark parked about two hundred
yards to the north. The skinny freak comes down the road
to meet them. Love he says.

Get that thing out of here this is an FFZ says Lance.

What are you talking about what's an FFZ says the surprised freak.

Free Fire Zone get it out of here.

What do you mean we have as much right Lance levels his
rifle at him. We're on an S & D. You're in B2. B2 is an FFZ.
Get out.

What says the freak.

I'm not kidding around says Lance.

Don't do it says Wind.

I'm gonna count to three says Lance.

Don't do it says Wind.

One two three says Lance he lets go with a shot and the
chimney of the Ark goes flying.

He shot my truck says the freak.

One two three says Lance another shot shatters the tail
light as Wind knocks his rifle down. The freak doesn't even
say anything he just gets his people together in about thirty
seconds the truck is moving out.

That's the way to do things says Lance. That's the way
to get results.

Yeah but I'm afraid we haven't seen them yet says Wind.

Shit. That's the kind of language people understand says
Lance.

Catsapandybangageleakysand says Cloud.

What's that.

That's the kind of language people don't understand.

That night The Monster catches fire. It's such a big fire
that the Volunteer Fire Department of Stamperville comes
to watch. By the time it's out The Monster is gutted. Then
the Volunteer Fire Department of Stamperville pitches in
to rip up the guts.

Wind is going back to the city anyway. Blossom Bud and Branch decide to camp in the clearing they break out a tent. Lance gets enough stuff together for a long backpack trip into the forest. Cloud hikes and hitches through the rain over to The River Queen to reclaim Eucalyptus. When he finally gets there after a two mile walk through a flooding rain he finds nobody's heard of Eucalyptus. There is no more Eucalyptus. There never was a Eucalyptus. Her name is Eve. That's what Eucalyptus tells him. Also Cloud discovers that people can't understand what he's saying to them. They take him to see Fatima. I think he's flipping out I'm really worried about him says Eve.

I'm not flipping out I'm lipping out. Bluh bluh bluh see I'm perfectly inane says Cloud.

What's your sign says Fatima.

My sign is your sign. Auld Laing. Neon that's my cosine. Something old and something new. Join the navy see the world sign us on. Except for my sinus I feel fine. How are you.

What's your birthday.

Cloud clutches his head. Too much nachas. Seven and seven is fourteen is the question period over.

You're a water sign The River Queen is always open to a water sign. Give him a berth says Fatima.

Happy birthday says Cloud.

Eve is staying with Buck. Eucalyptus doesn't exist any more. Cloud doesn't exist any more either. Cloud has burst. He stays in his bunk and cries a lot whoever he is. From this he understands he must be sad. At some point Dolly Dawn comes to visit she tells him about the redneck bar. We get a very enthusiastic crowd there she says. The Baba tells him a lot of nonsense. He tells the Baba a lot of nonsense this seems to disturb Dolly Dawn. Sometime before or after that he sees Blossom Bud and Branch. Blossom Bud and Branch have decided to stick it out at the settlement. They're going to rebuild. They've managed to get the regional Playflesh franchise and they're going to turn The Monster into a doll factory. They've taken out a bank loan and they're hiring labor from The River Queen. Maybe you'd like a job. Maybe Blossom's a slob. These people whoever they are he knows these aren't their real names seem to get sad when they see him. Why. Because he cries a lot. He likes to cry. They should try they'd like it too. The Missing Lunk cries. The Missing Lunk cries a lot. And when he doesn't cry he laughs. Or sighs or moans or roars or snores or something in between. One of the worst things about people is when they should cry they laugh and when they should laugh they do nothing at all. Cry more laugh more. He recognized The Missing Lunk on the last S & D Mission. He heard it coming out of Lance's mouth. That is what he heard was not The Lunk but the fact that it was Missing. That's when he decided to speak the kind of language people don't understand. If they don't understand it The Lunk can hide there. As soon as they understand it they hunt it down and then The Lunk is Missing again. At the first sign of a lurking Lunk they send out S & D Missions all over the place. This language that people don't understand is extremely stupid and nonsensical and is the language The Lunk speaks. This language is called Bjorsq. While Bjorsq is obviously inconvenient for many purposes it has one great advantage when two Lunks meet and speak in Bjorsq they understand one another perfectly. It's more than understanding it's as if they're singing a duet together as if they're hugging one another as if they're rocking in one another's arms responsive to every nuance of mood. It's a little like making love a coming together. Of course Bjorsq isn't very exact you couldn't write a text-book in it it expresses nothing with any definition but that's the price you pay. It defines little but it says everything. That's why you pay the price. It's not this or that object floating in the stream it's the whole force and direction of the stream the power that moves everything. The stream is feeling the medium of Bjorsq the language that people don't understand. This is the language he wants to speak. Until he can speak it he'll speak no other. He puts it other ways Bjorsq is a vertical language all others are horizontal. Bjorsq is a deep language all others are flat. Bjorsq is a window language all others are mirrors. Bjorsq is rhythmic the rhythm of your pulse the rhythm of the surf. All others are clopclop. It's the language of the map to The Ancien Caja whatever that is. He thinks all this is very clever. He thinks he has it all figured out. He won't speak the language that people can understand but he thinks it. He thinks it and that's the trouble. He's so smart.

    He stays in his bunk and feels the river rocking. The Thin King is dead. He talks to himself quietly bibbling babbling bubbling as the river flows by. He's pulled the silver rip cord
                lip cord slip cord
                            the Thin King makes no sense the Fat Queen say what it mean
                          the Fat Queen is flat
Fatty is a flatty oo ba doo
                  River Queen sea monster flat and fishy
    monsters get monsters Blossom Bud and Branch are having a
           they come to the weakly orgy Buck Buck mutants on the bounty
             monsters get monsters monsterspawn
                        mutants have more fun look flat feel flat be flat Blossom's flat with child oo ba doo oo ba dee
                  monsters get monsters Blossom is flatulent with child the world is flat and getting flatter
                      no harm no charm come fun come all
                  Flatima Buck Buck Buck Buck flat as a dollar bill Eve is flattered flatter and flatter by angels by freaks rednecks wetbacks drug zombies
                    no more Thin King
the Thin King was a failure
              time of the Flat Queen
                        flat as
cardboard stale beer old plastic slum linoleum

                                        flat as the

tundra
        flat as a corpse

Reflection on the mirror.
The mirror.
The mirror is double.
The mirror is ee/or.
The mirror is separation.
The mirror is painful.
The mirror is self conscious.
No more self no more conscious.
End of reflection.

    The Living Buddha is in town. The Living Buddha stops
here on his journey from Tibet to Staten Island.
    The Living Buddha is in exile an orphan of God. If The
Dalai Lama dies and someone else The Living Buddha becomes The Dalai Lama.
    When The Living Buddha dies someone else becomes The
Living Buddha a small boy somewhere in the mountains of
Tibet immediately becomes The Living Buddha. Then the
priests have to find him. That's how they found The Living
Buddha.
    Someone goes to see The Living Buddha. A small brown
man dressed in no special way greets him at the door. A
small man with very big feet. He has the friendliest smile.
He speaks no English. He grins. And he laughs. Or sometimes he makes other sounds he grunts he growls and as he
makes the Yak dung tea he seems to click. Or cluck. The Yak
dung tea is the only thing he seems to have of Tibet. Yak

dung tea is not tea of dung but tea held together in a brick by dung of Yak. This gives it a special flavor. I don't remember the flavor but I remember it was special. Meanwhile The Living Buddha seems to gaze at him with great curiosity brown eyes blazing at him with curiosity and good humor. It's a curiosity that makes him feel confused and light. A curiosity he would like to oblige of which he has no fear. He's not afraid. That alone is almost enough to make him cry. He wants to speak but he has nothing to say and The Living Buddha doesn't understand English. They drink their tea and The Living Buddha makes sounds at him. He grunts he clucks he giggles. He giggles like a demented child. It's very disconcerting and at the same time very funny. Finally he takes an orange and peels it clucking his nonsense. Grinning he hands me half the orange. As he eats he starts throwing the pits at me laughing and giggling he keeps throwing them at me till finally I start laughing too. Then he starts making funny gestures with his hands. He gestures giggles nods at me. Gestures giggles nods. Gestures giggles nods till I catch on and imitate the position of his hands whereupon he throws himself backward explosion of delight rocking back and forth gusts of laughter for a minute it looks like he's about to do a backward somersault. And that's not all after that he gets up and teaches me a little dance step a dance with the same odd hand gestures both of us laughing so hard by now the laughing turns to crying and then the crying turns to laughing and back to crying till there's no difference between laughing and crying if I don't stop I'm going to piss in my pants I don't stop I piss in my pants. I piss in my pants and that just makes me laugh harder sobs of laugher arpeggios of laughter rainbows of laughter I can feel my bowels loosening I'm going to take a shit then and there unstoppable it's so funny I'm howling shrieking blubbering I thought I was going to puke. And there we were laughing and crying together. Me and The Living Buddha. The Living Buddha nodding at me in great approval. This is what happened many years ago when I met The Living Buddha. He died in Staten Island several years back. Stomach cancer. If you don't believe me look it up it was on the front page of *The Times.* I saw it in the paper and I was sorry. Now somewhere in the mountains of Tibet there is a young boy who is The Living Buddha. The priests can't go find him because of the red regime. What nonsense. A peasant boy The Living Buddha. Om mani padme hum.

PALESTINE

Interruption. Discontinuity. Imperfection. It can't be
helped. This very instant as I write as you read a hundred
things. A hundred things to tangle with resolve ignore before
you are together. Together for an instant and then smash
it's all gone still it's worth it. I feel. This composure grown
out of ongoing decomposition. So far there are fifty-eight
words in this composition. I go to Israel where I am well
received one because I have connections Sukenick was the
name of the archeologist who discovered the Dead Sea
Scrolls his son is also an archeologist a general an important
minister two because this novel is based on The Mosaic Law
the law of mosaics or how to deal with parts in the absence
of wholes. So here I am. Two things. I have to go visit The
Wailing Wall. I have a private audience with Golda Meir.
I'll keep you informed. Now close the book go to the store
buy a box of matzos and eat some. With chicken fat and a
little salt. Butter will do. It will help you get the essential
taste of my Israeli experience. While you're there you could
bring back a little lox and bagels for me yet it wouldn't
kill you. In Laguna Beach you can't get you tell them lox
they tell you keys. What do you want I wouldn't go on this
way if that Arab wasn't such a lousy shot. They wouldn't
tolerate this kind of writing under a Nixon administration.
What Arab. The one where Rosy Grier broke his neck
when he tried to assassinate Kennedy after the California
primary two shots and all he could do was nick an earlobe
Sirwhat. That's why Robert favors high collars and wears
his overcoat turned up. Yes Robert that's how he's known
to his intimates Bobby's for the press. Got those matzos

yet what you didn't even leave. All right I'll stop here and wait for you to get back. Only for you. You're back. Good to see you what took so long. Now go take a nosh and we'll continue. Mazza. You know what that means in Italian. Mishuganah. Nuts. So you think I'm crazy well let me tell you if those slugs had buried themselves in Robert's brain everything would have been very different. That sentence should be better. Should be should be. You think I'm nuts if those slugs buried themselves in Robert's brain it all would have been very very different. If. If I had leaped out of bed and started writing instead of screwing around half the morning it probably would have been a better sentence. God alone knows what heavens we lose each slovenly minute. On the other hand who knows what salvations we might pluck from circumstance if we were open to the unknown. Oh well time to each lunch I guess. In Israel there are places where the jungle comes down to the sea and this is where I like to each lunch. They have beach cabanas there you can have a long leisurely meal cooled by the breezes coming in from the Mediterranean as you watch the submarine excavation projects. Despite the jungle and the deserts inland Israel has perfect weather all year round it has to do with air currents generated over the Afar Triangle on the Red Sea. It can be a hundred ten in Cairo in Jerusalem it will be a balmy seventy-five. And no smog. After lunch I catch a caravan across the Jordan where I want to visit some of my Arab friends besides I always enjoy the camel ride. So high. And so bumpy and precarious like something out of Coney Island. And the neck bobbing around in front of you like a big camel hair penis. Also the Arabs are so friendly and hospitable they keep embracing you and stuffing you with dates and baklava I shouldn't say Arabs we're all Palestinians now Arabs and Jews. Semites. Brothers. Of course I can't understand what they're saying it sounds something like Ychachach hassiss quoacha I try to keep my end up anyway and respond as well as I can. Thus we have long sympathetic conversations that often end in laughter and embraces.

Ou sacha jabb yotzi.

Nacha. Joss yissaj chorosis.

Vass nichayim sliss bachti noss spissel jachachiss. Giggles. Slaps on the back. Pass the water pipe. The friend I most particularly want to see today is the astronomer Yitzak

Fawzi. Whether Yitzak Fawzi is actually an Arab is as many things about Yitzak Fawzi not entirely clear. He may be Jewish but if Jewish why live on the East Bank. Yitzak Fawzi's explanations about this are not entirely clear partly because he doesn't speak English very well understatement of the year. One suspects Sufism somewhere in the background but again this is not entirely clear. I swing down off the camel in a narrow cobbled street lined by white cubes connected by high white walls. Yitzak Fawzi comes out in his white turban his white beard and his long white robe Saalem he says I return his greeting. We settle in his garden among murmuring channels of bubbling water whose geometry outlines an intricate star under the shade of cypress and palms on the stone table a jug of clear water. Yitzak Fawzi pours me a glass of water Pliss he says I thank him What we talk he says I shrug and smile.

Today we ask what is the matter says Yitzak Fawzi.

I've always wanted to know I say.

Yiss. What is the matter. This is the same question as what is the spirit. But opposite.

I see.

Yiss. Is matter spirit or is spirit matter which do you think.

I'm not sure.

Or is the same. Yiss. Corpuscle or plasma. Or the both. Blood.

Blood also maybe. Blood also is the matter. And the spirit. The physicists tells us it is the both. This is contradiction. What is real. Particles or waves. Corpuscles or plasma. Not the both.

Not both.

Not. Not particles. Particles are statistics. In the principle they do not exist as the individuals only in abstract in aggregate the principle of uncertainty. This is the matter. The matter is particles. Particles do not exist. Not only do they not exist also they are discontinuous in the principle the principle of probability. There is no real connection between one body and another. Between one event and another. There is a gap. Material equals corpuscular equals body equals statistical equals discontinuous equals unreal equals mechanical equals missing a dimension equals flat. But does it. In the principle the more you look the less you

find basic principle of quantum mechanics. The observer
becomes a function of the observed. Thus discontinuity is
a function of the observer is it not. Thus the bankruptcy
of empiricism is it not.

Possibly.

Possibly. Yiss. But the waves are not the matter. The
waves are the laws. The waves are the fingerprints of the
spirit on the blank page of matter. In the principle the
waves exist. The physicists tell us the waves are individuals
not abstractions. The waves are continuous. They fill the
gaps. They are the missing dimension. They are connected.
Certain. Improbable. The waves are the improbabilities of
the unknown that one perceives through intuition. Intro-
spection. Empathy. A sense of beauty. Through imagination in other words. The philosopher is the musician of the
improbable. Here where I live the beat of the ocean waves
is the one rhythm against which all other rhythms occur
including the deep rhythms of the blood and the breath.
The effect of this basal rhythm the long Pacific swell as
Winters has called it is to measure and magnify all other
rhythms all other events thus life is music here on the coast
of Israel. The deep rhythms of the body and the large
rhythms of the ocean seem to have a certain affinity so
that when the one are attuned to the other you enter into
a peaceful state that resembles a waking dream try counting
a hundred ocean waves you can't without an enormous
effort of will to avoid autohypnosis. The water of the ocean
is quite incidental to the rhythms of the waves the water
does not move the wave moves through the water and leaves
the water behind perhaps the material of the body is quite
incidental to the rhythms of the body the rhythms of life
which may move through the body then leave it behind. Up
the coast in Oregon a rock weighing one hundred thirty-five
pounds was thrown by a wave ninety-one feet above the
water to fall through the roof of Tillamook Rock Light in
Scotland a breakwater of two thousand six hundred tons
was removed as a unit by the waves of a stormy ocean since
the world's coastal population is constantly increasing we
can expect that within the next century somewhere a wave
will occur at least equalling the one that swept the shores
of the Bay of Bengal in 1876 leaving two hundred thousand
dead. The improbabilities of the unknown. Yiss. But the

waves are not the matter. The waves are the spirit. The matter
does not exist. That is the matter. That we imagine that it
does and don't imagine that it doesn't do you follow. As if
it exists without us without imagination that is the matter.
A loss of imagination. And what is imagination but the waves
of the spirit and what is the spirit. And how do we speak to
it. And where is it found. And why do we come to the Holy
Land. Rehovot Yehud Ariha Nabulus Tammun Karkur
Ya'bud Qalqilyah Ashqelon Bayt Lahm Yerushalayim. One
reason we come to the Holy Land is that there is now reason
to suspect it is the site of The Ancien Caja there is much still
buried here finds that may change the whole concept of the
past and of ourselves as Professor Sukenick has so dazzlingly
demonstrated through the famous Scrolls and that is the
reason for the submarine excavations off the coasts of
Quintana Roo Bermuda in the Bahamas. At the same time
working on the ancient Mayan inscriptions and codices.
Secret code on the leopard's fur the turtle's shell. The
language that people don't understand. Keyhole into the.
Butterflies. We come up out of a pyramid at Chichén. Jungle
storm of yellow butterflies. A clearing off one edge of the
site the yellow flutter thickens clots a grove of Eucalyptus
the source of all yellow butterflies. According to one theory
Sapiens and Neanderthal developed independently of one
another Sapiens in Europe and Africa Neanderthal in East
Asia the latter with a more advanced civilization before his
extinction providing our ancestors with the impulse to
higher cultural development a kind of missing link see J. E.
Weckler *Scientific American* December 1957. It is improbable that some specimens of the Neanderthal type low skull
jutting brow ridge broad nose muzzle mouth crossed the
landbridge to Alaska thence down the west coast to escape
the extinction of their Asian brothers. But not impossible.
In the space between nothing is impossible. The gap. The
blank space the clean slate. Where the terror is. And where
dreams condense like clouds in an empty sky. Civilization
comes down to a man staring at an empty page. Ravings. I
have important practical things to do. I have to get my car
fixed. I have to call my agent. Here in Israel we have no
need of cars. Or of agents. Automobiles have long been
exiled from the cities and towns where transportation depends on various beasts of burden camels burros oxen. There

are even a few llamas to be seen and modern experiments are
underway with giraffes and zebras which in fact antedate the
use of the horse in Africa and the Middle East. We have an
extensive intercity monorail system and colorful barges make
their way among the canals. Environmental planning is
largely given over to the artists with the result that the native
beauty of the Holy Land has been preserved and even
heightened. The prestige of novelists along with other artists
is such that no intermediaries are needed between ourselves
and the public and we have the means to produce and dis-
tribute our own work which is in constant demand. Artists
are recognized as the creators not only of esthetic works but
of reality itself all scholars scientists and rabbis are acknowl-
edged as artists each working in his appropriate sphere even
politics is considered to be a certain kind of art. I live in a
kibbutz called The Wave. The Wave is situated beside the
sea and our main ritual activity is surfing. Surfing is practiced
by all the kibbutzim save the aged and infirm children begin
to surf at the age of three or four and we have many octe-
genarians who are still active surfers. Surfing is of the nature
of a sacrament for us it attunes us to the cosmos and gives
every man and woman direct access to that union with
nature so sought after by the sages through the ages. Giving
oneself up in harmony to the swelling wave is like returning
to the bosom of our mother the sea. Surfing also keeps us
in touch with the immateriality of the material for such is
the nature of waves which move through the water and
constantly leave it behind. Waves are also the nature of
physical life whose cosmic energy moves through the material
of the flesh and leaves it behind the scientific basis of these
genetic rhythms has been expounded to us by our great
microbiologist Dr. Frankenstein whose researches have un-
locked the secrets of life itself. The kindly if eccentric Dr.
Frankenstein who has taught us how to create ourselves in
finer and finer harmony with the rhythms of the cosmos
is universally regarded here in Israel as a father and a great
sage indeed some regard him as a visitor from another part
of the cosmos though he gently ridicules this notion certain
of his eccentricities lend it a certain amount of credence in
particular the strange appearance of his fingernails which
are long and claw-like and painted in V shaped stripes of red
white and blue and also his habit of breaking into an incom-

prehensible gibberish some say a higher language without
warning or transition in the middle of a sentence. It is from
Dr. Frankenstein that we learned the basic sexual nature of
energy enabling us to eroticize all of our pursuits. Great
slow waves of rhythmic energy while at the same time
escaping that frantic sexuality which acts as a morbid irritant
beyond the borders of Israel. The phone is ringing. I answer
it a suave female voice tells me the President is on the wire
it's Robert he wants me to visit him at the Western White
House what he calls his heliocopter is already on the way.
Before I know it I'm in the heliocopter a small trim machine
skimming over the cliffy coast to Newport Beach a rich
yacht suburb of the jet set halfway between Los Angeles
and San Clemente it sets me down on the Presidential beach
Robert is dressed in a bathing suit and earmuffs he's been
surfing as we all do in Israel when something heavy is on our
minds. A word about the earmuffs rumor has it that Robert
is seen so often in his red earmuffs because they transmit
messages from some occult source this is definitely not the
case there is nothing weird involved except perhaps a kind
of innocent vanity I'm happy to clear that up. Robert is
troubled about sexuality he wants to know how we handle
this matter in The Wave not so much on a personal basis
you understand but on the level of policy and metaphysics.
Of course I'm always glad to toss this kind of thing around
with you but what particular aspect did you have in mind
I say.
    Robert fixes me with two dead blue clots of jelly of course
this is not for publication he says.
    Of course.
    We might begin with the question of jealousy.
    That is at the heart of the matter as one might expect.
Many researchers have tried to evade this problem but any
results that do not include jealousy as one of the fundamental
variables will be hopelessly jejeune. There is not one recorded
instance where this did not have to be dealt with. Unless of
course you eliminate feeling feeling of any kind and then you
are well on the road to eliminating sexuality itself in fact
we have developed an equasion. $L = P/J$ this is known as The
Law of Inconstancy. Love equals passion divided by jealousy
obviously a very unstable condition. Among its correlaries
is that jealousy bears a positive relation to love the more the

love the more the jealousy. The only way to escape this consequence is to deny the fundamental importance of sexuality itself and drift off into philosophical abstractions an option today reserved to only the most puerile theorists. Add to The Law of Inconstancy one the fact of differing interests between any given love partners and two a basic conflict of interest between the sexes and we begin to see the dimensions of the problem. Eve of course comes to Israel with me. We join the community of The Wave together as we have been together many years and whatever fluctuations in our relation made all major moves together. Between us there is much love and there is much pain it is not a glib relation. According to The Law of Inconstancy the love is not constant it comes and goes in rhythms in waves also the pain is not constant. Rebekah. Oh these suntanned softic Israeli girls let us not underestimate the sun. The sun is energy it works through the flesh it energizes it sensualizes it is as though the whole body were a genital. These suntanned girls running around The Wave always in their bikinis generous bodies. A whole generation of boys and girls generous to their bodies generous with their bodies generating great waves of sexuality the generous generation of course they're working through their own hangups I'm not aware of that yet. So Rebekah. Inevitable. The crest of a long wave I ride on till it breaks. At the same time great waves of pain between Eve and myself fights threats mutual hysterias. This cannot be evaded and there is no solution. No solution except The Law of Inconstancy $L = P/J$ the greater the love the greater the jealousy therefore by definition the love is capable of containing the jealousy even as the wave of pain is breaking the wave of love is gathering. When a couple in The Wave becomes mature enough to understand The Law of Inconstancy they are considered to be ready for the marriage rite which we call Eating Newton's Apple. Eating Newton's Apple implies a passage from innocence to understanding it means that you are down to earth that you have your feet on the ground it means you are a serious person it refers to Newton's sudden comprehension of gravity when he saw the apple falling from the tree it's what we call the fortunate fall. There are very few couples that have eaten Newton's Apple. I have to admit that I haven't yet done so though I've had a few bites out of it. This is something most of us find hard to swallow I guess.

Robert nods. I know that he not only understands what I'm
saying but that he knows it before I say it that he is even
perhaps putting it into my mind through telepathy since I
know that I don't know it before I say it and don't know
where it comes from. This thought is further borne out by
Robert's next question which echoes exactly what is in my
mind at that instant What about orgasm. What about orgasm
this is precisely the central question the question on which
our entire civilization stands or falls is it because of his
Catholic background that Robert has a knack for these
theological considerations. The tradition of the Scholastic
Fathers accustomed to those minute theoretical distinctions
which though absurd to the layman shaped the course of
European history. There is a state known to scholars of the
subject that they call Pure Horniness. Pure Horniness is a
very dangerous condition. You think about Rebekah you
forget about feeding the cat. You forget about Eve. The
family the job the welfare of the community the whole
thing cat and kibbutz. Probably you forget about your
own well-being you even forget about Rebekah herself.
Rebekah isn't the point you're just in this pure state that
Rebekah isn't even enough to satisfy this is the PH Factor
and there's nothing you can do about it except maybe fuck
yourself to death. In The Wave we can see one another's
auras there's something about the Holy Land conducive to
seeing haloes all those old paintings. When the PH Factor
is present in Rebekah her aura is a deep blue flare she's
aflame she inflames others pretty soon the whole settlement
is on fire. People want to die. They want to stop being
people. They want to be meat they want to be things. You
want Rebekah to be a thing. You don't want any personal
considerations any sign of humanity enrages you makes you
cruel you want to kill her. Pretty soon everything is shot to
hell the energy released in this kind of spasm is enormous
ecstatic and terrible. A transmutation occurs not unlike that
in an atomic explosion the delicate balance of personal and
social forces held in suspension that we call civilization explodes in a moment of frenzy rape cruelty murder and
collapses into the lower level of organization characteristic
of dead matter Hitler's Germany. Eros provokes Thanatos.
Or so they say. It's fucking that opens Pandora's box.
Orgasm is the first gasp the first gasp of insatiability that

only ends by ending the unbearable tension between matter and spirit between life and death. In my relations with Rebekah there are three phases The Phase of Cruelty The Phase of Imagination The Phase of Illumination. In The Phase of Cruelty Rebekah is an idea an idea of which her breasts and buttocks are correlaries and her vagina the proof you might say a carnal idea that is an idea of carnality like a sexy ad a salacious photograph. She is an idea for me I am an idea for her. Ideas start in the head. They are analytic. They are discontinuous with the object. They are a priori in the sense that you lay them on the object she lays her idea on me I lay my idea on her the mode is rape. This is the empirical tradition mind rapes nature manipulation exploitation control. Inevitable. Incredibly erotic. Rebekah is a slave. Make me do things. Hurt me. My penis is a weapon. She submits to my power she comes like a string of firecrackers I have three orgasms at a shot we make love all day we're insatiable. It occurs to me we're looking for something the essence of meat. There is no essence of meat. That's why we're insatiable. That's Subphase One. Subphase Two is Fesselation. In Fesselation there is a great deal of oral play on both sides. There seems to be an idea abroad that sperm might be the essence or barring that that a carnal sacrament might be possible we might in some sense be able to eat one another the spirit is actually immanent in the body therefore etcetera. But despite our holiest perversions there is no real connection between one body and another. This is the matter. Discontinuity. Thus Subphase Three is inevitable. Sodomy. I keep her in a state of perpetual excitation satisfying myself between her buttocks. Since the closer we come to continuity the further we are driven from it the only way to achieve union is for one of us to in effect cease existing to become a pure object a thing ecstasies of sado-masochism ensue. Hurt me. Make me fuck dogs. I want to be a prostitute. I want to die. After coitus all men are sad. Naturally. With this kind of coitus. Let's move on. In this phase Rebekah's aura is a huge ragged flare a brush fire everyone feels it she turns everyone on we decide to hold open house a constant stream of men singly in large groups file through her legs the neighbors are beginning to complain one day we're making love I put my hands around her throat If you come I'm going to kill you I say she moans and starts to come my hands tighten next thing I know I'm in a new phase. That's the closest I'll ever come to murder. I'm in shock for three days. In the next phase we don't make love. We meditate. This is The Phase of Imagination. We contemplate one another's beauty we withdraw into ourselves I try to imagine what she feels like You know what Rebekah says one day.

What.

I don't know you.

Check. Tentatively gradually we start making love again only we don't go all the way we stop short of orgasm. We neck a lot and play around I feel like a kid again. We're using what we call The Rhythm Method in The Rhythm Method you try to sense your partner's rhythm you don't try to lay anything on her you get attuned it's like a new combo tuning up if you don't get the rhythm you don't make the love. You wait. You come to the point of orgasm and then withdraw you withdraw back into yourself you contain the energy instead of getting it off this fills you with a lot of energy the only trouble is it drives you crazy. All that energy instead of streaming out through your genitals detours back up into your head and presses against the top of your skull you feel like you're going to start levitating any minute this is a good time to eat Newton's Apple. If you don't fly off into the stratosphere at this point you become hyperconcious. You begin to see. When you begin to see you begin to cry. This happens to Rebekah and myself at exactly the same moment What's wrong I say.

What do you mean.

You're crying.

So are you.

How come.

I feel sorry for you. How come you.

Ditto. This is where The Rhythm Method gives way to The Wave Theory. Let's plot this on a graph get a piece of graph paper. Draw two waves Wave A cresting in the trough of Wave B Wave B cresting in the trough of Wave A. Now extend both waves across the graph paper as they advance the waves begin to coincide trough to crest the point of coincidence we call X. X equals the unknown. When two people's rhythms coincide perfectly we can't know what happens this is what we call love. Love is a state that we can't know we can only experience it but then experience is a form of knowledge is it not. True it is not abstract knowledge it is the initial form of knowledge but perhaps it is also the final form of knowledge. This is a possible correlary of The Wave Theory I must go down to the beach and think about this in any case let's push on. X equals the unknown. There are two things we can say about it first if a is the energy of A b of B and x of X then $x = a^2 \times b^2$ and that's a lot of energy second at point X all sorts of improbable connections between the two of you become luminously obvious this is The Phase of Illumination you may throw away the graph paper. In The Phase of Illumination orgasm is what I can only term a musical experience. In this phase we may say that after coitus all men laugh. Gently. The consequence of this kind of orgasm is harmony as opposed to the cacaphony inherent in the sadomasochistic type. Luminous Orgasm is an important objective in the teaching of the new science of Psychosynthesis. We can also determine according to the laws of Psychosynthesis from the number and quality of improbable connections that become luminously obvious between partners at the moment of Luminous Orgasm how long a given relation can harmoniously last. In the case of Rebekah and myself it is the length of one Luminous Orgasm our crests can coincide perfectly only once the perfect wave has come and is gone forever we know it immediately no hard feelings smiling we wave goodbye. You can talk all you want says Robert. But it all comes down to social justice and in practical terms that requires power. That's the only way out. Fear times anger equals power. What do you mean I say. I'm not against social justice I'll prove it. ANNOUNCEMENT. WILL EVERYBODY PLEASE CLOSE THIS BOOK AND WRITE OUT A CHECK FOR FIVE DOLLARS TO THE AMERICAN CIVIL LIBERTIES UNION. REPEAT. IT IS FORBIDDEN TO CONTINUE WITHOUT MAKING A CONTRIBUTION TO THE ACLU. Hurry up what's taking so long. Ah there you are can we proceed. Good. While you were gone I met Rebekah. I'm sorry you didn't get to meet her but that's what you get for being so slow. It seems she's going out with a boy named Phillip Phillip was the name of my grandfather. Rebekah was the name of my grandmother what do you make of that. Can time run backwards that is the question

for today. Yiss. I'm waiting for a call from Yitzak Fawzi he
said he'd call me yesterday or today. If he doesn't call me
today maybe he'll call me yesterday. That would be an
answer to the question. The physicists say it is not impossible. There are black holes in space anti-matter time reversed
electrons. Maybe everything is happening at once what then.
One vast coincidence. Here in Israel the extraordinary is
run-of-the-mill. We are capable of living in a state in which
certain things that have happened have not. At the same
time that they have. This is The State of Israel. If it is true
that consciousness affects matter by regulating entropy then
The State of Israel is a crucial factor. The way you enter
The State of Israel is through Psychosynthesis. In the
processes of Psychosynthesis as in the subconscious as in
the laws of physics there is no negation. Let me ask you
something I'm very curious about you. What are you feeling
now what is your life like. Can you describe it in a series
of equations. Each equation should include the term fear
thus failure plus fear equals despair love divided by fear
equals hate now drop the term fear. Thus failure does not
lead to despair love does not lead to hate you can look at
your life this way even though it is not this way. But once
you begin to look at life this way it begins to change do
you follow a change in the field of consciousness is a change
in the field of fact in one of the crucial factors in the field
of fact. Such a change is known as Reversing Your Electrons.
A reversed electron is a positron the physicists tell us that
a positron may go backward in time. Yiss. You are now
entering The State of Israel. But first you must visit The
Wailing Wall where you must mourn for everything that has
been lost. The Second Temple thanks to the Romans. The
Library at Alexandria thanks to Heliogabulus. The Mayan
codices thanks to the Catholic missionaries. The tablets
buried under the statues of Easter Island thanks to the
missionaries again. A generation of Jewish intellectuals
thanks to Hitler. The Chamber of Horrors. The Chamber of
Horrors is a memorial and reminder of the camps what they
did there is an essential part of everyone's education and
helps you develop a strong stomach. Auschwitz as a vaccine.
Many people catch the disease you have to be hard as hard
as whatever it is that hurt you. You have to become what
hurt you. Or else. Or else it may hurt you again. They are

making a mistake. Those who prefer to forget are also making
a mistake. The camps are not something you can negate as
if they never happened. The negative when it is developed
becomes the positive like what America did to Viet Nam.
Thank god that stopped the moment Robert took office
otherwise we might have had eight more years of genocide
plus a collapse of civil rights plus a subversion of civil
liberties plus government spy networks sabotage teams black-
lists of enemies official harassment political trials rigged
elections strangely convenient assassinations of course you
will think me mad admittedly I exaggerate but still. The
Weimar Republic and all. When we speak of this phenomenon
we are speaking of disease you understand. Mental disease
a disorder of the imagination only the mind can deal with
the mind only the imagination can deal with the imagination
thus Psychosynthesis. A way of curing the disease without
catching it. A way of things happening without happening.
A way of dreaming without dreaming. A way of going mad
without going mad. We deny nothing. We incorporate the
negation in the affirmation. Auschwitz did not happen even
though it did. Israel exists even though it does not. Atlantis
did not exist even though it did. I WANT TO KNOW WHAT'S
GOING ON IN THE BERMUDA TRIANGLE. WHY DON'T
THEY INVESTIGATE THE HUGE SUBMERGED WALLS
VISIBLE FROM THE AIR. WHY DO AIRPLANES DIS-
APPEAR THERE. WHY DO FUNNY THINGS HAPPEN
WITH TIME. WHAT DID THEY REALLY FIND ON THE
MOON. WHY DON'T THEY RELEASE THE REAL IN-
FORMATION ON FLYING SAUCERS. WHY DON'T
THEY TRACK DOWN THE SASQUATCH. THE ABOMI-
NABLE SNOWMAN. WHAT ABOUT THE BLOBS IN
TEXAS. WHAT ABOUT CAYCE. WHY DID THE SCIEN-
TISTS CRUCIFY VELIKOVSKI. WHAT ABOUT MESSAGES
FROM OUTER SPACE. WHY DON'T THEY TELL US THE
TRUTH. You have to incorporate the negation in the affirma-
tion. But before you can do that you have to visit The
Wailing Wall. You have to mourn for everything that's been
lost. You have to remember everyone who's died. You
have to think about every tortured child. You have to con-
sider the inevitability of pain. You have to ponder cruelty.
You have to meditate on despair. You have to remember the
exile and that we're all in exile. You have to weep for the

orphans and remember that we're all orphans. And it's not enough to think about all this you have to imagine it. You have to live it. You have to get down on your knees and roll your head in the dust and if you have to scream then you scream. A cleared square. A big white wall. People kneeling praying dovening crying kissing the wall. The Temple. There are other worlds than the world we know and though they are not real this world is not final. THEY ARE REAL. There are two necessities. There is inner necessity and outer necessity. When the wave of inner necessity coincides with the wave of outer necessity another world is psychosynthesized this is what we call The Moment of Luminous Coincidence. The State of Israel is a Moment of Luminous Coincidence. Without The State of Israel life would become inconceivable it would lose a necessary dimension it would become flat we would all become Nazis. Yet the trouble is that The State of Israel is itself almost inconceivable. First of all they speak Hebrew there a language most of us don't understand. And even those who understand it complain that they can't understand the peculiar form of the language spoken by the natives the Sabras. And the Sabras themselves have such difficulty communicating with one another in this language that they always have to resort to the common dialect. Wisdom is dangerously close to nonsense why is that. THERE ARE IMMORTALS AMONG US EXTRA-TERRESTRIALS THERE IS A SECRET LANGUAGE I WANT MY MOMMY DA DA CA CA CACACAC BJORSQ. A reporter comes to interview me. He's from an American paper. He wants to know about the quality of life in The State of Israel. How many suicides do you have among males between the ages of twenty and thirty.

I don't know.

What percentage of the population votes in major elections.
I don't know.

What is the current rate of exchange between dollars and shekels. Between shekels and gold.

I don't know. I don't know.

How many members in your average mean family.

Our families aren't mean.

Don't kid around. What is your gross national product.

It's not gross.

Cooperate.

Do you want the quality of life or the quantity of life.
We want yardsticks. Most people in The State of Israel
feel good when they get up in the morning. Yes or no.

Well it's hard to say a lot of it depends on dreams and
the weather also the time of month probably a lot of people
I know have told me they have certain physical rhythms
that are relevant personally for me it's partly a question
of whether I've made love the night before however I don't
think you should feel bad about feeling bad when you wake
up that just makes you feel worse whereas these things tend
to unkink themselves if left alone the other day for example
when I got up my left ear was twitching.

No examples. Yes or no. People in your State breathe
deeply and chew their food in a relaxed manner. Yes or no.

Well that depends on several things.

Yes or no yes or no. Most people in your State are content to sit on their porches in the evening and chat. True or
false.

Ronald Sukenick. Private. 065-26-6564.

True or false true or false. By and large adults in your
State smile when they see lovers pet stray cats and remember
their own childhood in a pleasant manner when they watch
children playing. Right or wrong.

Ronald Sukenick. Private. 065-26-6564.

People in your State want their mommies. Right or wrong.

Private. Private. Private. We are currently working on the
general equations that would express happiness and unhappi-
ness in terms valid for all individuals in all states. Yes people
in our State want their mommies. And we get them too.
Our mommies are nicer than your mommies. A RADIO
BROADCAST IN TEXAS WAS SUDDENLY RECEIVED
FIVE YEARS LATER BY RESIDENTS OF LONDON.
THREE LEGGED ALBINOS SEEN HOPPING AROUND
IN THE MIDWEST. MEAT RAINS FROM THE SKY. AN
EXTRATERRESTRIAL SATELLITE DETECTED CIR-
CLING EARTH. STARS ARRANGED IN SEMAPHORE
MESSAGES. There exists a passion for comprehension
which like a passion for music opens the possibility that
therefore all the information was not present in the initial
state of the universe implying a complementary universe
when you are there it is not when it is there you are not
axiomatically beyond prediction or even comprehension.

The scientific apparatus the litter of books their places
marked with whatever flotsam comes to hand feathers bits
of string playing cards twigs paychecks whose disposition
drives the accounting department bananas Mozart's *Voi che
sapete* comes softly through the loudspeakers. I can recollect
his fingernails his manner of speaking but what he looks like
whether or not he wears glasses or has a beard I simply can't
remember no one can. As to his background we know nothing
except of course his professional achievement the Weimar
Period neoindustrialization the cybernetic revolution the
Manhattan Project genetic microbiology and of course his
theories about rhythm worked out on bongos and conga
drum after his trip through the Amazon jungle. Some say
he is one of The Seven I don't know anything about this.
And if I did I wouldn't tell you. I detect strong remnants of
a Brooklyn accent but perhaps that is only because I come
from Brooklyn. His sense of humor is proverbial especially
the Eulenspeigellian stories about his practical jokes at Los
Alamos in the old days when he made a hobby of penetrating
the locks and alarm systems of the highest security areas
leaving tiny notes before carefully resetting and relocking
all security mechanisms. His rambling monologues are
punctuated by an intermittent static of nonsense which
he seems not to notice no one knows what to make of this.
As he talks you find crazy things going through your head
a piece of vermicelli preserved in glass till it begins to twitch
with its own motion. His first name seems to be Phillip
though he tells different people different things. Dr. Frankenstein do you plan to promote the kind of neoindustrialization with which you are identified in Europe and America
here in Israel.

The answer is yes and no that kind of development is of
course necessary and at the same time brings its typical
problems which are all too familiar to all of us on the other
hand here in The Holy Land we have perhaps other oppor-
tunities that might render the techniques of neoindustrialization wastefully crude electrify the nimbuses improve the
sewers in Jerusalem as the witty poet remarks MAKE DOO
DOO CAT CAT CGA TCA TGC ATG CAT CAT CAT CAT
CAT. At first I thought he was merely calling his cat a big
furry handsome looking fellow black with white breast and
paws that I hadn't noticed before and indeed the animal at

this point leapt purring into his lap It was this big furry fellow that gave me one of my key insights into genetics namely if you call a cat by its right name it will come but mutations are nonsense out of phase with the cosmos a filthy mass that moved and talked but note at this point we have already eaten the apple no way out but further in we move through and beyond sexuality from the creative act to creation itself we become as little children as tiny foetuses as egg and sperm as chromosome and chromosome only mutation amends mutation GOO GOO CA CA GA GA GUGUGUGUGUG UGU GUG UGU GUG GUU GUC GUA GUG valine one of the many interesting developments was that the three letter words that we thought were nonsense in the four letter code turned out to be information we didn't yet understand when we discovered the twenty letter language GUC CAU CAC UUA BJORSQ sometimes it happens that first you discover the word then you discover what it means thus Schrodinger's wave equation developed on esthetic principles before the phenomenon it described was known to exist this accounts for my fascination with pangrams VEX'D PIG HYMN WALTZ FUCK BJORSQ suppose mathematics and poetry are both systems that reflect the nature of the cosmos then the word becomes the Word there is sufficient linguistic potential in the four letter genetic code of a human cell to store a thousand large text-books suppose that language is the connection between spirit and matter after all you do it I do it the birds and even the bees do it I mean use language nicht wahr.

Yes father.

In fact I see no reason not to suppose that the rhythms of sex are a kind of language rhythm in general the vibra-tion modes of drumheads of atoms the genetic code might itself be expressed in three quarter time what is the rhythm the cosmos it don't mean a thing if it ain't got that swing he picks up a turtle shell beats on its two ends as if it were a bongo drum Something I picked up in Yucatan where they use it among other things to send messages through the jungle.

Yes father.

Already we can synthesize certain DNA molecules of course the human chromosome is ten thousand times larger but the era of genetic engineering is not too remote not too remote and once we can produce controlled mutation do you understand we will have the power both to create life and control evolution we will synthesize a new race a superman.

You've already bungled once father.

More than once but one day I shall succeed. Superman.

Will he be a good boy father.

If you give him a nickel he'll be a good boy he gives me an indian head nickel you don't see those much any more what do you say to your Granpa.

Thank you Granpa IN COSMIC WAVES FROM THE PLANET KRYPTON A NEW WORD IS COMING A WORD THAT WAS HERE BEFORE THE FLOOD THAT WAS ALWAYS HERE A WORD THAT SAYS ALL THOSE STRANGE THINGS THAT WE DO NOT UNDERSTAND OR LIKE TO THINK ABOUT. Miss pelling zard is pelling zif sole cism sol ipsism be. Schism of gism. Fork you. Double double talk and trouble zee prize you pay. For good granma. Bad lang witch. Ize brake you sin tax. In no sense. A blisskrieg yet. Mit schlag bubola. O joie thou trivial spicemonger thou with spredden snatch. Pig bag. Unwholly. To see through the mirror look through the pane. Thatsa bout tit. Meeches on saddy. At dipitches. Here cumz motion pigture excrement. Into the cuttingroom out with your heart. Speak up son stop mumbling.

Ex cuseme I 'mnotto geth erI don 'twan ttob einh ismo vie.

Now now wipe your nose why don't you want to be in his movie whose movie.

Hesca re demI 'malli nli ttl epi eces.

You've been to see Frankenstein and it scared you to bits. Tch tch tch she feels my forehead. You're feverish take your temperature. Just what frightened you so much.

Id on 'tkn ow.

Here come to Tanta Goldie he's a little cold isn't he a little inhuman did he fill you with all his crazy theories that's just talk.

Ifee llik esuc hafi lth yme ssaf lopaf ailu re.

No no don't listen to him with all his talk about superman you're not a flop. He thinks so much about superman he forgets about you and me and who is this superman anyhow. Who says he's better than us. Maybe he'll be worse.

Th enwha t'sth eans wer.

Come give Tanta Goldie a hug one answer is nicer mommies. If you'll promise to stop crying I'll tell you a few things.

All right I promise.

First of all an answer I don't have. A question I can give you an answer no. Let me tell you something I once asked Einstein. I was questioning his effort to bring the laws that govern atomic particles into line with the general theory of relativity. What good does all this theory do I finally asked him unless we find a way of incorporating it into our experience. My dear skeptic he said. Albert Einstein. He was standing as close as you are to me. My dear skeptic you are perfectly right. Only experience can restore that lost synthesis which analysis has forced us to shatter. Experience alone can decide on truth.

And while we're waiting.

And while we're waiting faith. Faith enough to forge an art of experience to deal with our fate. As Martin Buber told me not long before he died you have to become an illogical positivist. In The State of Israel you become an illogical positivist. Now will you be a good boy.

Make me happy and I'll be good.

Well I'll tell you what if you try I'll try now give your Tanta Goldie a kiss because she has to go.

One more question Prime Minister Meir what is The Ancien Caja.

Ah The Ancien Caja. The Old Box The Ark The Solar Barque. Everyone has his own version.

I don't understand.

More I can't tell you it's a State Secret. Oyf a mayse fregt men nisht keyn kashe.

What's that mean Granma.

That's the Secret Language. What we call the mame-loshn.

But why do you have to speak the Secret Language when I don't understand it.

Because do ligt der hunt bagrobn don't ask so many questions.

But Grandpa says it's stupid to speak a language no one understands.

Khazerei. A kadokhes vel ikh im gebn. You don't have to

understand it do you understand everything you remember. You have to love it and feel it. I see our time is up. Thank you.

Thank you Mrs. Meir. Walkin with ma baby on the side of San Francisco Bay I'm listening to the blues I'm about to have A Moment of Luminous Coincidence I feel it coming on it's coming together JESSELONECATFULLERJESSE SEARLYLIFEWASSPENTRAMBLINGBETWEENGEORGIA TEXASANDCALIFORNIAWHEREHEEVENTUALLY SETTLEDALONGTHEWAYHELEARNEDSPIRITUALS BLUESRAGSANDHILLBILLYSONGSHEADAPTEDT THEMALLTOHISTWELVESTRINGGUITARSTYLEBUT ITWASNOTUNTIL1950THATTHEDECIDEDTOSEEKOUT WORKASAMUSICIANHEENCOUNTEREDTROUBLE FINDINGRELIABLESIDEMENSOHEBECAMEAONEMAN BAND playing all the instruments AT THE SAME TIME I'm sitting in Laguna Beach with the cat on my lap listening to The San Francisco Blues by Lone Cat Fuller AT THE SAME TIME trying to finish my novel AT THE SAME TIME trying to forget about it I pick and open a book at random Fuller Buckminster quotes Fuller Margaret all attempts to construct a national literature must end in abortions like the monster of Frankenstein things with forms but soulless and therefore revolting we cannot have expression till there is something to be expressed AT THE SAME TIME trying to forget about it a trip a bar in a distant city turns out to be called Frankenstein franks and steins AT THE SAME TIME this morning's mail with an article by Ihab Hassan on Prometheus Frankenstein Orpheus AT THE SAME TIME thinking when you try to sew Orpheus back together what you get is Frankenstein AT THE SAME TIME hearing on the radio Lon Chaney just died a few miles away from here in San Clemente AT THE SAME TIME reading this record jacket thinking yes ramble around settle in California pick up this and that adapt it to your style without sidemen the novelist is a one man band playing all the instruments AT THE SAME TIME playing along on a kazoo AT THE SAME TIME moving to San Francisco AT THE SAME TIME entering The State of Israel AT THE SAME TIME orchestrating the whole thing toward those Moments of Luminous Coincidence when everything comes together AT THE SAME TIME AT THE SAME TIME sorry to leave Southern California the sun the waves the mother tongue another bungled paradise AT THE SAME

TIME happy to be heading for San Francisco another chance
AT THE SAME TIME tying up my novel AT THE SAME
TIME my life is unravelling AT THE SAME TIME the novel
is bungled fragments stitched together AT THE SAME TIME
everything is seamless perfect not because because because
but AT THE SAME TIME playing the blues letting it go it
is as it is. Another failure.

FICTION COLLECTIVE

Books in Print:

Searching for Survivors by Russell Banks

Reruns by Jonathan Baumbach

Museum by B. H. Friedman

The Secret Table by Mark J. Mirsky

Twiddledum Twaddledum by Peter Spielberg

98.6 by Ronald Sukenick

Statements: New Fiction, edited by Fiction Collective Authors